Shauna continued to [...]
glass front door into [...]

A familiar vehicle pulled up [...] heart to skip a beat. When Kent Chapman stepped out of the car, she found herself in a semi-hypnotic state. *What in the world? Well, this is a pleasant distraction.*

Shauna opened the front door and let him in. "I don't believe it," she said with a cool grin. "How did you figure out where I worked?"

"Where you work?" He looked confused.

"How did you find me?" She couldn't help but wonder, though the fact that he would take the time to find her workplace warmed her heart.

The puzzled look never left his face. "Find you?"

"Yeah. How did you know which day-care center to look for?"

"Shauna, I. . ."

"You could have just called," she whispered, looking around for Mrs. Fritz. "Not that I'm not happy to see you. I am. I really am. But our director's not really keen on strangers coming into the facility. Just the parents."

He had a curious look on his face, one she could not seem to read. For some reason, he looked nearly as surprised to see her as she did to see him. Something about all of this just seemed. . .wrong. Off.

"Shauna, you—you don't understand," Kent stammered.

"What do you mean?"

"I mean. . ." He reached out his arms to scoop up an all-too-familiar youngster. "I *am* a parent. And I'm here to pick up my daughter. That's all. To be honest, I didn't have a clue you worked here."

Shauna stared in disbelief at the child in his arms and fought to catch her breath. *You've got to be kidding me.*

"Charity?"

JANICE THOMPSON is a Christian author who resides in south Texas with her husband and grown daughters. Her entire family is active in ministry, primarily praise and worship. Janice is the elementary director at her church and devotes much of her time to children. She seeks to make a difference in the lives of those she comes in contact with, and hopes to spread the gospel message through the stories the Lord gives her.

Books by Janice Thompson

HEARTSONG PRESENTS
HP490—A Class of Her Own
HP593—Angel Incognito
HP613—A Chorus of One

Sweet Charity

Janice Thompson

Heartsong Presents

This fun-loving story about a young woman's love for children is dedicated to my daughter, Megan, who works as a private nanny. Megan, your face lights up every time a child enters the room, and that warms my heart. May you always remember that each child is a special gift from God, even the ones who try your patience.

A note from the Author:
I love to hear from my readers! You may correspond with me by writing:

Janice Thompson
Author Relations
PO Box 719
Uhrichsville, OH 44683

ISBN 1-59310-782-X

SWEET CHARITY

All scripture quotations, unless otherwise indicated, are taken from the Holy BIBLE, NEW INTERNATIONAL VERSION®. NIV®. Copyright © 1973, 1978, 1984 by International Bible Society. Used by permission of Zondervan Publishing House. All rights reserved.

All of the characters and events in this book are fictitious. Any resemblance to actual persons, living or dead, or to actual events is purely coincidental.

Our mission is to publish and distribute inspirational products offering exceptional value and biblical encouragement to the masses.

PRINTED IN THE U.S.A.

one

"Shauna, you're going to be working with the two-year-olds."

"Two-year-olds?" Shauna Alexander gazed into the kind eyes of Mrs. Fritz, the day-care director.

"How do you feel about that, dear?"

Shauna hesitated a moment before answering. Caring for children that young didn't exactly fit into her plan, but then again, how hard could it be? She tried to sound self-assured as she spoke. "I usually work with the older ones, but I'll be happy to give it a try."

Her recently acquired degree in early childhood education had given her a well-rounded knowledge of children, but she had hoped to focus on four- and five-year-olds. Then again, maybe this was God's plan. Surely she could handle toddlers—with a fistful of prayer and a good, positive attitude.

"I'm sure you'll do fine," Mrs. Fritz said with a smile. "Children are children, regardless of their age. And you seem young at heart. That's a quality the younger boys and girls will really relate to. You seem like a lot of fun."

"Thank you. That's really sweet." Shauna smiled as she pondered the director's words of encouragement. Mrs. Fritz was not the first to make note of her youthfulness, and Shauna saw this quality as a potential asset. She hoped so, at any rate. Her experience had been limited, at least so far—though her hopes and dreams of working with children never wavered. Someday, she would have a day care of her own, if everything went as planned.

5

"Let me show you around, honey," the older woman said with a smile. "I just know you're going to love our facility. And I'm sure it won't take you any time at all to fall in love with the children."

Shauna couldn't help but feel hopeful as she followed Mrs. Fritz through the halls of the child-care center. *What an adorable facility.* Despite its age, the Hiz-Kidz Christian Day Care proved to be quite colorful and creative. In fact, the sights and smells tickled her senses and caused her to want to be a part of this wonderful place. The rooms overflowed with active little ones. Their childish chatter, though loud, stirred Shauna's imagination and warmed her heart.

"This is our infant room." Mrs. Fritz pointed toward a large room filled with uniform white baby beds. The walls, soft powder blue, were hand-painted with clouds and stars. The whole place was a dizzying mixture of aromas—some good, and others not so good. Shauna looked around curiously, wrinkling her nose. *Ah. That would explain it.* In the corner of the room, an older woman was changing a youngster's diaper. The little one let out a squeal, fighting the routine.

"We take them from six weeks up to about a year in here," Mrs. Fritz explained, clearly oblivious to the noise. She pointed at one of the workers, who held a sleeping infant in her arms. "That's Lila. She's got three children of her own. And over there is Nora. She's been with us for sixteen years."

Shauna nodded in the direction of the two women. Lila, a lovely young woman with olive skin and a broad smile, returned the gesture, but Nora, the older, diaper-changing woman, gave her a stern once-over that sent a little shiver down Shauna's spine.

Goodness. I don't want to get on her bad side.

"We always use two teachers in the infant room," Mrs. Fritz

explained. "The babies are quite a handful."

So are two-year-olds.

Shauna traipsed along behind Mrs. Fritz as they made their way to the kitchen. A young woman, probably in her early twenties, dished out plates of macaroni and cheese and green beans. She had shocking red hair and earrings that lined each ear all the way up.

Mrs. Fritz made the introductions, clearly not focusing on the girl's appearance. "Ellen, I'd like you to meet Shauna. She's going to be our new lead teacher in the two-year-old room."

Shauna groaned internally as the words were spoken. *Two-year-olds. Help me, Lord.* She smiled in the young woman's direction and tried not to let her disappointment show.

Ellen looked up from her work just long enough to verbalize a quick greeting. Her dazzling smile convinced Shauna they would be friends. *Thank You, Lord. I needed someone my own age here.*

Mrs. Fritz led the way through the other classrooms, each ablaze with activity. A finger-painting project appeared to be underway in the four-year-old room. Messy paints in bright blues and reds adorned every chubby finger. The five-year-olds were out on the playground—some swinging, others arguing with one another over who would get the next turn on the slide. The older, after-school crowd was distracted by a video, though many of them seemed to be content to tease and torment each other instead of paying attention to the film. By the time they reached the two-year-olds, Shauna felt a bit dazed. Would she really be able to take this much activity?

"Here are your little charges." Mrs. Fritz entered a colorful room with pastel rainbows painted on the walls. From the rainbow hung an array of bright silver stars, each one printed with a child's name. Shauna helplessly gazed around as she counted. One, two, three, four. . .eight, nine, ten, eleven, twelve. Twelve? How could she manage with so many? Their voices rose and fell as the teacher, a young woman with a knotted brow, worked to calm them.

"This is Julia." Mrs. Fritz pointed to the frenzied-looking young woman with sheer exhaustion etched on her face. "She's not able to teach after this week. You'll be taking her place. That is, if you're still interested."

Shauna looked carefully at the smirk on Julia's face and tried to read her expression. The young woman seemed to be trying to tell her something with a glance, but what? *Run as fast as you can from this place!* Was that it? Then again, could she really base her decision on a look?

Shauna glanced over the roomful of children. How difficult could they be, anyway? Most of them were absolutely darling with their colorful clothes and whimsical voices. She felt herself drawn to them immediately and could see herself here in this place, teaching them and loving each and every one. After all, there was no obstacle so large that love could not overcome it.

"Charity, turn back around!" Julia scolded a particularly beautiful little girl with blond curls who sat in the corner. "You still have three minutes left." She tapped her watch, clearly for effect.

"Three minutes in the corner?" Shauna asked, amazed. "What has she done?"

"What hasn't she done?" Julia mumbled as she reached over to pick up some toys from the floor. She shook her head and pressed a stray hair behind her ear. "You name it, she's done it."

"She's a precious child." Mrs. Fritz gave Julia a puzzled look. "One of God's little blessings."

"Humph." Julia turned the opposite direction.

How awful! Shauna shook her head, suddenly determined. What kind of a woman would take an innocent little girl like that and glue her nose to the wall?

"I'm still interested." She faced Mrs. Fritz with a renewed anticipation. "And I'd be happy to start on Monday."

As they turned and walked from the room, she felt sure she heard Julia's mumbled response: "Good luck. You're going to need it."

❧

Kent Chapman looked around the small church office, trying to take it all in. Nothing in his twenty-seven years of living could have prepared him for the challenge he now faced. And yet all of life's many lessons, good and bad, seemed to have come together, forming a road that led him here—to the pastor's office of Grace Community Church.

Interim pastor.

None of his friends from high school would believe it, even if they had sobered up a bit. After all, he could scarcely believe it himself, in spite of his radical conversion and years of working in public relations. Even his mother, his greatest fan, seemed a bit dubious at the prospect. Kent understood the uncertainty, especially in light of his years of rebellion as a teen. *What in the world is God up to here? Why would He pick me, of all people?*

And yet here he stood, a nervous twenty-seven–year-old, in the tiny pastoral office of Grace Community, ready to—at least temporarily—fill the shoes of Pastor Meeks, a man of God the congregation had loved for thirty-five wonderful and fruitful years.

"Just six months, Kent," the board members had implored. "Six months will give us time to bring in a new man, someone who can put a fresh face on things. That's all we need."

Kent had argued, as much with the Lord as with the leaders of the medium-sized congregation. How could he possibly fill the shoes of someone like Pastor Meeks? And how could these godly men overlook his years away from the Lord as a teen, entrusting him with the position of leadership? And yet they had. How could he argue with that? And why would he want to, when God so clearly laid the idea of ministry on his heart?

"You've worked so well with the youth group." Kent smiled as he remembered the kind words the men had spoken over him. *"And you know so much about what draws them in. That's what we need around here, at least for a while—a young fellow like you to bring us into the twenty-first century. We'll find the man for the job, but in the meantime, you'll more than do. Besides, we need a familiar face in the pulpit, someone the people can relate to. It's going to be mighty hard to adjust to someone brand new after all these years. Transitions take time."*

Yes, they do. If Kent understood anything at all, he understood that. This certainly wasn't the first time he had been asked to take the reins and move into a new position of leadership. His mind reeled with all of the changes he'd been through over the past several years. . .transitioning into the role of "head of household" after his father died. . .opening himself up to a relationship with his stepfather, Andrew, after his mother remarried. . .entering into a relationship with the Lord after being away for so long. . .stepping into marriage with Faith at age twenty-three, and the birth of their daughter just a year and a half later.

Transitioning. . .

Kent shuddered, remembering. Accepting Faith's death still presented the most challenging shift in his life. For months after the tragic accident that swept her away, he struggled to maintain his sanity, his love for life, his faith.

Faith. . .

If not for his daughter. . . He smiled, thinking of the beautiful little girl awaiting him at home. If not for her, he would surely have lost his reason for living. But she kept him going, day in and day out. And he had an obligation to raise her as Faith would have wanted—in the arms of her family and friends and in a strong church with plenty to offer its congregation.

With renewed zeal, Kent gazed across the office once again. "I need to be positive. God has placed me here for some reason, and I'm going to give this my best shot."

In the meantime, potty training awaited. Kent glanced at his watch then raced to pack his briefcase and head home.

two

Shauna left the day-care center after the brief tour, content to believe the Lord had just offered her an amazing new opportunity. She pressed aside any fear. If Daniel could face a den of angry lions, surely she could face a roomful of toddlers.

After all, she had prepared for this day for years. Why begrudge it just because the Lord had shifted gears a little? Two-year-olds couldn't be that difficult. And besides, she would one day start her own center—in God's timing, of course. Until then, she would use every moment to acquire practical knowledge, which she would some day put to use with her own little ones.

As she crossed the parking lot, Shauna felt her lips turn up in a playful smile. Could life get any better than this, really? "Thank You for the job, Lord!" Surely He had provided it, just as He had provided the direction she needed during her freshman year in college. No one could have been more surprised than she when the Lord gave the instructions to settle into an elementary education degree program. But now, years later, she could certainly see God's hand at work in every detail, including this new position at the day care. Two-year-olds or no two-year-olds.

Shauna climbed into her white Saturn, deep in thought. Just as she started to turn the key in the ignition, her cell phone rang. She scrambled through her cluttered purse to find it. "Hello?"

"Shauna Alexander?"

"Yes."

"This is Bill Conner from Computers Unlimited. You left your PC with us a couple of days ago?"

"Yes, that's right." Shauna turned the key, and the engine started smoothly. She balanced the phone on her shoulder as she pulled away from the Hiz-Kidz Day Care. "Is it ready to be picked up?" *I need to send Joey an e-mail.* Thoughts of her boyfriend suddenly made her sad. She missed him so much.

"Yes, ma'am," the voice on the phone continued. "We replaced the fan. The machine had been overheating, causing it to lock up on you. But it's all taken care of now. Good as new."

"How much?" The dreaded question.

"Four dollars for the part, but then there's the labor charge of forty-nine ninety-five to put it in."

"Naturally." Shauna sighed as she pulled onto the busy street. "How late are you guys open?"

"We're here till five."

She glanced down at her watch, nearly driving the car off of the road. 4:36 p.m. "I should be there just in time," Shauna said, as she fought to steady the wheel. "So don't close without me, okay? I really need my computer tonight."

"We'll be here," he said. Then, with a click, he disappeared.

Shauna tossed the phone into her purse and headed out onto the interstate.

❧

Kent Chapman pulled his Jeep Cherokee onto Interstate 45 on Houston's north side, headed toward home. When his cell phone let out a loud ring, he struggled to pull it from his pocket.

"Hello?"

"Kent?"

He recognized his mother's voice immediately. "Hey, Mom. How are you?"

"Fine now," she said. "But I'm glad you didn't ask me that an hour ago. We ran into a little dilemma at the bookstore this afternoon."

"What happened?" Kent knew his mother's love for Bookends, the store she had managed for the past several years.

"One of our coffee shop customers carried a cup of coffee out into the store and had a spill. She managed to wipe out an entire shelf of inspirational fiction. Took us nearly an hour to figure out which books we could save and which had to be tossed."

"I'm so sorry to hear that." He was sorry for several reasons, but primarily because he knew his mother would have to bear the cost of the books.

"It's not really that big of a deal." She sighed. "To be honest, I was more worried about being late to pick up that beautiful granddaughter of mine."

Kent could hear his daughter in the background, chattering away. "Sounds like you got her."

"Yep. She's chattering my ear off right now."

He glanced at his watch. "Well, I'm on my way to your place now. I know you're probably worn out."

"I am, but I love spending time with her. You know that." She disappeared for a moment then returned with laughter in her voice. "She's telling me what she wants for dinner. Chicken nuggets."

Kent groaned. "Not again." Just then, another call beeped in. "Hang on a minute, Mom." He switched to the other line and tried to figure out who it might be before giving a curious "Hello?"

"Mr. Chapman?"

"Yes?"

"This is Bill Conner from Computers Unlimited. We've finished upgrading your computer. You can pick it up at any time."

Ah-ha. Finally. "How late are you open?" Kent glanced at the clock.

"Five o'clock."

"Okay." He sighed and attempted to change lanes. "I'll be there in just a few minutes."

Kent clicked back to his mother. "Still there?" He could hear his daughter still chattering away.

"I'm here." His mom sounded a little weary. "She's wearing me out with a speech about some movie they watched in school. Something about a whale."

"Ah." Kent hesitated a moment, trying to exit the freeway. "Mom, I hate to ask, but. . ."

"You're going to be late?"

"I just got a call from the computer store. They're finished with my PC." Kent managed to work his way through the afternoon traffic as he headed onto the feeder road. Once he reached the intersection, he headed for the U-turn lane. "I guess it could wait till Monday, but I'd rather get it now. I sure could use it to get ready for Sunday's sermon."

"How long do you think you'll be? Should I go ahead and fix dinner for all of us?"

"I guess." He sighed as he turned the car in the opposite direction. "I'm really sorry, Mom. I know I depend on you too much. I'm working on that. I really am."

"Pooh. You know I love it. And so does Andrew. We can't get enough of you two. Haven't you figured that out by now?"

Kent smiled, comforted by her response and equally as

relieved that his stepfather shared in her enthusiasm. "I have. And I won't be long, I'm sure. I'll just swing in and pick it up and head right to your place."

"I'll have a big plate of chicken nuggets waiting on you."

Kent groaned. "Thanks a lot."

They said their good-byes, and Kent chuckled as he hung up the phone. His mother and stepfather had more than helped him through the past couple of years; they had truly supported him and encouraged him to put one foot in front of the other, day after day. "Lord, give them a double portion of Your blessing."

His thoughts shifted to the computer as he traveled south on the feeder road. With a new motherboard installed, the machine should be as good as new. At any rate, he couldn't afford to do without it much longer—not with so much at stake.

Kent drew in a deep breath and leaned back against the seat, deep in thought. In the two and a half years since his wife's sudden death, he had taken to journaling, writing down his deepest thoughts. They flowed out of his fingertips onto the computer. The keyboard felt natural to him, becoming a close friend and confidante. And now, with his new job at the church, Kent had another reason to rely on the machine.

Of course, with his computer in the shop, the past few weeks he had taken to scribbling down his thoughts on scraps of paper. However, short, choppy thoughts written down on tiny slips of paper never made for long, flowing messages. That wasn't to say he could deliver them in a flowing manner, at least not yet. But to try to put together a sermon without a computer seemed nearly impossible. Writing by hand had become, at least for him, a thing of the past. It felt too old-fashioned.

Mr. Twenty-first Century Pastor. Kent chuckled as he thought about what the teens at the church called him these days. They were fascinated by his ability to stay on top of the latest technology. The congregation had recently purchased an amazing video system, and their sound booth held one of the latest soundboards available on the market. Each week, the words to the praise-and-worship songs were flashed up onto large screens via an amazing computer system, which he had put together himself.

Yes, technology certainly intrigued Kent. In his heart, he knew that every bit of it could be used to evangelize—to reach the world with the gospel message. Why else would the Lord have given man the ideas for such items in the first place? These things were worthwhile, and he was more than intrigued. He was hooked.

If you're so up on modern things, why don't you just buy a new computer? That old relic doesn't even have a DVD-ROM. His heart quickened as he considered the possibility. Funny, every time he thought about purchasing a new machine, Kent almost felt sick. He had been using this one the night his wife. . .

No. I won't let myself think like that. It's in the past now.

He exited the freeway at Rayford Road and gave his watch a quick glance. 4:57 p.m. Only three minutes before the shop closed. Hopefully they would wait on him since they knew he was on his way. Kent whipped into the parking lot of Computers Unlimited, relieved to see another vehicle pulling up at the same time. "Looks like I'm not alone."

The young woman in the white Saturn hopped out of her car and sprinted toward the door. He quickly followed suit. Thankfully the door still remained unlocked. An anxious employee stood just behind the counter, staring at the clock on the wall.

"I'm here to pick up my computer." Both Kent and the young woman spoke in unison and then gazed at each other curiously.

He couldn't be sure who started laughing first, but both seemed just as quickly embarrassed by it. He smiled in her direction to put her at ease. "You go ahead."

"No, please. You go." She fumbled through her purse, coming up with a cell phone.

He shrugged and turned toward the counter. "Kent Chapman."

"Shauna Alexander." The young woman continued to struggle with her cell phone as she spoke.

Kent couldn't help but take notice. Though clearly a little younger than himself, she was awfully cute with her choppy, sandy-colored hair and bright blue eyes. She wore a pair of shorts overalls with a colorful shirt underneath. He guessed her to be in her early twenties.

What are you doing, man? You stopped looking ages ago.

"I didn't think I'd make it on time," she said breathlessly. "I was driving like a maniac on the interstate."

"I thought I recognized that Saturn of yours." He gave her a warm smile.

"Are you kidding?" She looked at him nervously. "I'm so sorry. I was just in such a hurry."

"Calm down." He chuckled. "That was my attempt at a joke."

"Oh." She leaned her elbows onto the counter and placed her chin in her hands, obviously weary. "I'm sorry. It's been kind of a stressful day. I'm starting a new job."

"Hey, I'm in a new job, too. What do you do?"

Just as she started to answer, two workers rounded the corner with PCs in their hands.

"Kent Chapman?" one of them asked.

"Shauna Alexander?" the other echoed.

Kent and Shauna looked at each other and erupted into laughter again. The computers were identical, right down to the make, model, and color.

"Could this get any more bizarre?" Shauna reached to pull out her checkbook.

"I doubt it." Kent shook his head as he reached for his wallet.

The two chatted as they paid for the repairs and then headed out to their vehicles together. To his left, the sun began to set, nearly blinding Kent with its glare.

At least he thought that dazzle came from the sun. Right now, he couldn't really be sure.

three

Shauna leaned back against her chair and surveyed the messy dining room table. "Everything was so good, Mom."

"Thank you." Her mother flashed a broad smile.

"I sure missed your cooking when I was in school," Shauna added. In fact, she couldn't remember when she'd had a better meal. No one could make chicken cacciatore like her mom, and Shauna had done without it far too long.

"Glad you enjoyed it. And I'm happy to have you here to cook for. After you moved up to College Station, I practically stopped cooking altogether. Your father and I ate out more than ever."

"Really? I didn't know that." She looked at her father intently for his response. Surely he would have one.

"Spent a fortune at that new diner on the interstate," her dad said. "And their food sure didn't taste like your mom's." He made a face.

"I'll bet." Shauna couldn't imagine how her father could have possibly adapted to restaurant food after years of eating like a king. She certainly understood the adjustment after shifting to college cafeteria foods.

"Didn't make a whole lot of sense to cook big meals just for the two of us." Her mother shrugged then reached to pick up Shauna's plate. "But now that you're back, I'll be cooking more. And who knows. . .maybe one of these days I'll have a houseful of grandbabies to cook for. Then I'll start fixing meals you can all be proud of again." She winked for effect.

Shauna groaned. "Oh, Mom."

"In the meantime," Shauna's father pushed his chair away from the table, "I'll probably take off another ten or twenty pounds. But don't worry about me. I'll be just fine." He rubbed his protruding belly, and Shauna laughed.

"Wouldn't hurt you to take off a few pounds," her mother said as she picked up his plate and added it to the stack.

Shauna snapped to attention as she realized her mother planned to do the dishes alone. "Oh, don't mess with that," she said. "Why don't you and Dad go watch some TV and let me get the dishes for a change?"

She felt a slight embarrassment at being waited on. Something about it made her feel like a child again. Returning home after college had its perks, to be sure, but she didn't want to take advantage of her parents in any way.

Mom's eyebrows elevated slightly. "Are you sure?"

"Of course." Shauna stood and began to clear the table. "You've both been so great to let me come back home. The least I can do is carry my own load. I don't want to be a burden, trust me."

"You could never be a burden." Her father stood from his place at the head of the table. "Never have been and never will be."

Shauna turned to face her parents head-on. "I just want you to know," she said, "that when my paychecks start rolling in, I plan to help out financially around here. It's the least I can do."

"Well now, I don't know about that. . ." her father looked a little uneasy with the idea.

Shauna crossed her arms as her thoughts flowed freely. "You guys paid all of my college expenses. That's more than a lot of parents would do. You put a roof over my head for years—before and after college. And you've helped me find a job."

"That's what parents are for," he argued.

"I know," she said, "but you know what the Bible says. . . 'From everyone who has been given much, much will be demanded; and from the one who has been entrusted with much, much more will be asked.' I've been given so much over the years, and I just want you to know how grateful I am—and how hard I'm going to work to become independent."

"No big rush, honey." Her father kissed her on the forehead. "We missed you while you were away, and we love having you home again."

"I know." She couldn't help but smile. "I love being here, too. But I really don't plan to stay forever, I promise. One of these days I'm going to have a family of my own." *Maybe it won't be too long.*

Her father pressed her into a warm embrace. "Don't be in any hurry, sweetheart. Just take your time until you're sure you've found someone who's worthy of you."

"Sounds like a typical dad comment." Shauna couldn't help but chuckle.

"Just doing my job." He gave her another hug then headed into the living room to read the newspaper.

Shauna whispered the next words, keeping her thoughts to herself, just in case. "I might have someone in mind, already." She glanced at her cell phone, which sat perched and ready on the kitchen counter. All evening long she had awaited a call from Joey. Would it ever come?

She thought about him as she cleared the table. She dreamed of him as she loaded the dishwasher. Their last few months together in College Station had pretty much sealed their relationship, at least according to her way of thinking. Sure, he was busy with his graduate classes, but soon. . .soon he would come for a visit, and her parents would see just how awesome he was.

She already knew, of course. He was pretty much everything she had always hoped for, right down to the amazing work ethic. His love for the Lord was evident, and he came from a great family. Though he hadn't expressed much interest in children, she felt sure he would come around. Most guys did, right?

As she worked, Shauna tried to imagine what her life would be like once she and Joey married. Would she stand at a sink like this, rinsing dishes? Would he stand beside her with a dish towel in hand, ready to help? Would they sit together in the living room afterwards, watching movies and talking about the day's events? Would they bathe their children then tuck them into bed each night? Shauna wrapped herself deep in thought as she considered the possibilities.

After finishing up the dishes, she set up her computer on the tiny desk in the bedroom she'd loved since childhood. Never one for technical things, she struggled to figure out which cord went with which machine. Finally, convinced she had the thing put together correctly, she sat in the chair and pushed the button, ready to get down to business.

As the machine booted up, Shauna fought the nagging feeling that something felt wrong. She couldn't quite put her finger on what it might be. Something just seemed amiss. Sooner or later it would reveal itself.

The computer went through an unusually slow process of getting to the main screen and even bypassed her password process. "That's odd." She tapped at the keyboard, growing anxious. After some time, the monitor lit up, though the colors on the screen threw her a bit.

"What in the world? Where is my wallpaper?" Instead of the usual blue sky and white fluffy clouds, an artistic rendition of the Last Supper covered the screen. "Is someone trying to tell me something?" Not that she minded, but those guys at the computer shop should at least ask before changing her configurations. She scrambled to find the familiar icon for her word processor. For some reason, it had been moved. In fact, nothing seemed to be in the right place.

"Looks like they added more than just a four-dollar part. They revamped the whole machine." Finally, after extensive searching, she found the necessary word-processing program. "It's about time," she mumbled. Looking at the blank screen, she began to type:

Dear Joey,

I have great news! I've got a new job at a day-care center. After searching for days, I finally stumbled across one that's not too far from my parents' home. That's a good thing, considering the fact that gas prices are so high. At least this way I'll keep my costs down. And here's a plus—it's a Christian day care. I'm so excited about that part because I can share my faith with the kids and the other workers.

The lady who runs the place is named Mrs. Fritz. Funny name, right? She's a little quirky, but, then again, so am I. She's from the "Old School," if you know what I mean. I hope that won't be a problem. At any rate, she seems to like me, and I'm pretty sure I can do a good job. I know I don't have much teaching time under my belt, but I'm sure the things I learned in college will prove to be valuable.

Speaking of college, how are your classes? I'm so proud of you for going on with your schooling. I don't know if I've said that enough, but I am. Just think, this time next year you'll have your master's. Wow!

I know you're swamped, but I'm still hoping you can come down for a couple of days next month. My parents are dying to meet you. They talk about you all the time. Well, I talk about you all of the time, anyway.

    Do you miss me? I think about you almost every day. I'm surprised I haven't gotten a letter from you yet. Did you get the one I sent last week? I've sent a couple of e-mails, too. I know you don't like the computer, so I guess we'll just have to stay connected the old-fashioned way.

    I guess that's all for now. I'm going to go to bed tonight thinking of you. Are you thinking of me?

                            Love and kisses, Shauna.

She saved the document and then reached up to print the letter. Leaning back, she let herself begin to dwell on Joey. He was two years older and working on his master's degree in psychology. His dark brown eyes were usually serious, but she didn't mind that. He was pretty nearly perfect in every other way. They shared similar values and aspirations. Their relationship had been as much academic as romantic, but she hadn't really minded. Too much.

Shauna looked at the printer suddenly, realizing the document hadn't begun to print. "What in the world is taking so long?" She immediately checked the printer folder on the PC, but was unable to find the appropriate driver listed. "What do those crazy people think they're doing?" Her frustration continued to mount.

Why in the world had she paid them before checking their work?

                         ❧

Kent turned on the computer, anxious to get busy on his sermon notes. It would take weeks—maybe months—to feel at ease in front of the congregation. The past several Sundays he had faced them with fear and trembling, anxious to hear from God and speak the appropriate message, but terrified he might not be able to speak a single sentence.

The computer seemed to boot up considerably faster than usual. "Wow. Looks like I really got my money's worth." The front screen appeared—a soft blue sky with white billowy clouds. "What's this?" Someone had messed with his wallpaper.

Well, no big deal, probably just some young technician with too much time on his hands. Kent opened the word-processing program and looked around for the familiar folder titled *SERMON NOTES*. Missing.

"Come on now." Agitation set in. Tampering with something that valuable was no joking matter. Kent began a frantic search of the computer's programs, looking for his notes. They weren't here. But lots of other things were. File after file of unidentifiable stuff. Love letters, college papers, personal notes, and. . .

"Ah-ha!" Letterhead. "Shauna J. Alexander."

Bingo.

four

As Shauna stood out on the back deck of her parents' home, she sipped a cup of hot coffee and spent a few minutes in prayer. The morning sun beamed high in the sky, causing a bit of a glare. Pinks and purples from the morning's sunrise had long since been replaced with a bright blue cloudless expanse. Shauna reveled in it a moment longer before picking up the portable phone to make the necessary call. She punched in the now-familiar number, prepared to do battle.

"Hello. Computers Unlimited." The voice on the other end sounded cheery. A rehearsed cheery.

Undeterred by the fellow's jovial attitude, she forged ahead. "This is Shauna Alexander," she started. "I'm. . ."

"Oh, Ms. Alexander," the friendly voice interrupted. "Say no more. We just heard from Mr. Chapman. He's got your computer."

She let out a sigh of relief, happy to know she wouldn't have to come out swinging. "I was hoping you'd say that."

"We're so sorry about the mix-up." Genuine empathy filled his voice. "The technician apparently confused the tags on the two machines. An unusual mistake, at least for us. In fact, I can't recall when it's ever happened before."

"Hmm, well. . ."

"He's terribly sorry," the man continued. "At any rate, Mr. Chapman's coming at ten thirty to drop off your PC. Any chance you could come at the same time? Save him another trip?"

"Ten thirty?" Shauna glanced down at her watch. It was already nine forty-five. For a moment, she thought about saying no, but then remembered Kent Chapman's deep green eyes. She didn't want to be the source of agitation to those kind eyes. "I'll be there." Shauna groaned as she hung up the phone. With a bit of frustration over losing yet another day to this problem, she headed back into the house to pack up the computer. Again.

❧

Kent began the familiar drive back to Computers Unlimited, trying to hold his temper in check. "Lord, I have so much to do today. Please give me patience and help me not to overreact at the computer store."

He tried to push his emotions aside as he made the trip. With so little time before tomorrow morning's service, he certainly needed more than patience. He needed divine intervention. Especially after the night he'd had.

Raising a child alone might prove to be his undoing, especially when it came to sleep schedules. Whoever said toddlers slept soundly hadn't met his daughter. She managed to stay awake until the wee hours most every night then awaken with the dawn, raring to go. "How long can she keep this up?" Surely things would change soon. He prayed.

Kent yawned and tried to keep his wits about him. As he pulled into the parking lot of the store, he noticed Shauna Alexander's white Saturn. She stood next to it, sunlight streaming through her short blond hair. Today, she wore a bright yellow T-shirt with a rubber duck image on the front along with a trendy pair of jeans. As he pulled up next to her car, she waved and smiled.

For some reason Kent's nerves kicked in just as he opened the car door, and the only word that could come was a shaky, "Hey."

"Hey to you, too." Her smile broadened, and he couldn't help but grin back.

"You stole my computer." He waggled his finger in her direction.

"No, *you* stole *my* computer." She crossed her arms and pretended to glare.

They both chuckled. "I'll be glad to finally get mine back, to be honest." Kent admitted. "I've got less than. . ." he glanced at his watch, "twenty-four hours to prepare a sermon."

"You really are a pastor." She looked more than a little surprised. "I guessed as much from some of the files I found on your computer."

A sigh escaped his lips. "I'm not used to the title yet, to be honest. I'm still on a learning curve, trust me. You have no idea."

"Still, that's very cool."

As she gave him a look of admiration, he felt his cheeks flush a little. "Don't get me wrong," he added quickly. "I love it."

"Oh, I'm sure it's great. A lot of responsibility, though. You're pretty young to pastor a church, but I guess you hear that a lot."

Kent took a minute to explain his situation. "I've gone to the same church since I was a kid. Our pastor just retired, and the board asked me to fill in until they found a permanent replacement."

"Ah." She nodded. "So you really are on a learning curve, then." Her eyebrows elevated slightly as she added, "I know what that feels like, trust me."

He couldn't help but wonder at her cryptic comment but didn't ask for an explanation. "I worked in the youth department for about three years," Kent explained, "but hanging out with teens is a lot different than facing a congregation full of people of all ages."

"I'll bet." She grinned. "That would scare me to death. I have enough trouble getting up in front younger people. Do you get nervous?"

"Maybe a little." He gave a helpless shrug. "But every week gets a little less nerve-wracking. Tomorrow will be my third Sunday in a row. And no one has left the church yet. That makes me feel a little better."

Dimples appeared as her smile widened. "Well, you'd better get home and get busy. You don't want to lose any parishioners because you stood in the parking lot all day gabbing."

No, but I sure wouldn't mind standing here a little bit longer to talk to you.

ɤ

Shauna couldn't figure out why her cheeks warmed as she talked to Kent Chapman. Probably just the late summer heat. She opened the trunk of her car so that the computer exchange could take place and then thanked him as he placed the PC inside her vehicle.

"I'm so sorry this happened." He spoke as if he had caused the problem. "I hope you didn't have to drive very far to get here."

"Oh, it's no problem, really," Shauna said. "I don't live far, and I didn't have any big plans this morning. Just need to get some lessons ready for Monday. And besides, it's certainly not your fault. Just a fluke."

"Right. A fluke." He smiled warmly.

She couldn't help but chuckle as she confessed, "You should have seen my face when the computer booted up and I saw that painting of the Last Supper. It really scared me. I thought maybe someone was trying to tell me something."

"Maybe they were." He shot her a lopsided grin. "You never know."

She nodded. "Maybe. The whole thing seemed a little suspicious. And I really got worried when I stumbled across those sermon notes, I don't mind telling you. I thought maybe the Lord was trying to get through to me in a new way."

He groaned and pressed his palm to his forehead. "You didn't read them, did you?"

She shrugged. "Sort of. I hope that's not a problem."

Kent's face tightened in obvious embarrassment. "I'm just not very good at putting my thoughts together on paper. At least not yet."

"Could've fooled me. I especially liked the one titled 'The Valley of the Shadow.'"

His gaze shifted downward. "That actually came from a journal entry I made during a horrible period in my life," he said. "But then you probably already know about that, too. You seem to know everything about me."

"Not really," Shauna said, suddenly self-conscious. "I mean, I wasn't trying to pry. I was just trying to figure out whose PC I had, that's all."

"I'm just kidding." He flashed a warm smile. "And besides, I know a few things about you, too."

"Like. . . ?" Shauna suddenly grew nervous, wondering what secrets her computer had revealed to this young pastor.

"I know you went to Texas A&M."

"That's right." *I'm safe so far.* "Best school in the country."

"Some would debate that, but I'd have to agree with you," he responded with a smile. "And I know that you wrote a terrific paper on teaching techniques for Pre-K students."

Her jaw dropped. "You read that?"

"I skimmed it," he confessed. "Intriguing. Carefully researched and well written. Convinced me."

"Good grief. What else?"

"Somebody named Joey Something-or-other up in College Station has been getting a lot of mail from you."

"Okay, that's enough." This guy had really overstepped his bounds now. She slammed the trunk closed. "My love life is none of your business."

"I'm sorry." He spoke with sincerity. "I really am. I was just looking for a name—trying to figure out whom the computer belonged to. Same as you. That's all."

"Right."

"Right," he echoed.

"Well, everything's straightened out now." Shauna gazed intently into his green eyes. "So I guess I'd better get back on the road. I'm supposed to meet my mom for lunch." She walked around to the driver's side and opened the door. He followed her and held the door open until she was safely inside.

"My parishioners thank you," Kent said with a tad bit of dramatic flair. "I have a hard time putting together my sermons by hand."

"No problem."

"I didn't realize how much I relied on my computer until I had to do without it. I really depend on it—and on the Internet. I guess it's right, what the kids say about me. I really am a twenty-first century pastor. I need all the modern conveniences to survive."

"Twenty-first century?" Shauna had to wonder what he meant. "Is that some sort of a tag or something? Your logo?"

"It's kind of a joke," he said with a laugh. "It started when I set up an Internet server at our church—Grace.com."

"Grace.com?" She grew more confused by the moment.

"I pastor Grace Community Church," he explained. "We're near downtown."

"Oh, I've heard about that one," she said. "You guys are really involved in the community, right?"

"Yes." He smiled. "And I'm particularly interested in using technology to reach out to the unchurched. Anyway, I came up with the screen name '*21stcenturypastor*' awhile back. One of the teens gave me that label after I preached a message to the youth group last year on relevance."

"Sounds like you've been preaching longer than three weeks, then."

He nodded. "I guess God's been getting me ready for a while now. Just didn't see it at the time. Like I said before, it's one thing to share in front of a roomful of teens, another thing altogether to stand in front of people of all ages. Teens are a little more forgiving when you make mistakes." Kent smiled, remembering. "More prone to make fun of you," he was quick to add, "but less prone to hold it against you."

"Come on now," Shauna said, feigning offense. "We're all forgiving. Just don't worry so much about what everyone thinks."

"I try to stay focused on what the Lord thinks," he said with a nod. "But thanks for the reminder."

"No problem." Shauna stood in silence a moment as she looked him over. This very contemporary looking twenty-something certainly didn't fit the typical pastor mode, but stranger things had happened. Why wouldn't the Lord use him to lead a congregation? Hadn't He chosen Shauna to work with two-year-olds?

"It's all still new to me," Kent continued, oblivious to her thoughts, "but I enjoy it, especially getting to know the people."

"Do you like the preaching part?" Shauna asked, genuinely curious. "Are you good at it?" She clamped her hand over her mouth, embarrassed she had phrased the question in such a way.

He laughed. "I do like to preach. Surprisingly. And people tell me I'm not half bad behind the pulpit, to answer your last question. Probably a little better at the public speaking part than the putting notes together part. Somehow when I stand up in front of the people, the words just seem to flow. Never could figure that out."

She grinned and nodded. "Well, maybe I'll have to come and hear a sermon or two before I draw any conclusions."

"Better come soon then," he explained. "I'll only be preaching a few months—just till the church locates a real pastor. I'm the in-between guy." His eyes lit up with a fire as he continued to speak. "But I love the fact that God could use someone like me—someone who has made mistakes then returned to the Lord—to speak to the lives of people. To give them hope. You know?"

Shauna nodded. With passion like his, why would his church need to look for someone else? "I'd like to come." *Did I really just say that?*

"Great!" He smiled broadly, and his green eyes twinkled a bit. "I'll be looking for you." He closed the door and waved a final good-bye. As Shauna pulled away, she couldn't help but look into her rearview mirror. *Mr. Twenty-first Century Pastor is awfully cute.*

Stop it, girl! What do you think you're doing? Somewhere in College Station a young man named Joey might someday ask her to marry him.

five

"Do you have anything for a headache? I think I have a migraine." Shauna asked the question, though she knew all the pain reliever in the world wouldn't cure her aching head.

"Tough day, huh?" Ellen asked.

Shauna rubbed the back of her neck and rolled her head from left to right trying to stretch the tenseness out of her muscles. Nothing seemed to help. "Man, I had no idea kids were this difficult. Is it too late to change my major?"

Ellen looked a little puzzled. "You've already got your degree, right?"

"Yeah," Shauna mumbled. "I was just kidding. But I really do need something for this headache, if you've got it."

Her new friend opened her purse and pulled out a giant-sized bottle of pain reliever. "I always keep this on hand," she said with a smile. "Never leave home without it."

Shauna nodded sympathetically. "I just wish someone had told me," she muttered. "That's the least they could have done." She glanced over at the table where her students sat, eating lunch. At once, she spotted a problem—and not an unusual one. "Charity! Stop throwing your food at Clay. Behave!"

"I behave, teacher." With a look of mischief in her eyes, the child turned back to the table.

"I see you've gotten to know Charity," Ellen spoke quietly, eyebrows elevating slightly.

"Why do you think I have this headache?" Shauna swallowed the tablets Ellen placed in her outstretched palm without even reaching for a glass of water. She turned back toward the table just in time to see the rambunctious youngster pinch the little girl next to her. "Charity!"

"No me!" the youngster said, shaking her head. "I no pinch her." Her blond curls bobbed back and forth with her denial. Dinah, the little girl next to her, erupted into a fit of tears. Soon two or three of the others joined in, probably as much out of sympathy as anything else.

"Is she always like this?" Shauna whispered to Ellen.

"No, not really. Sometimes she's worse."

Shauna rubbed her aching brow and prayed the day would come to a quick end. She headed over to the table, trying to calm the children down. "Let's all sing a song," she said cheerfully, breaking into, "This is the way we eat our lunch, eat our lunch, eat our lunch." By the time she got to, "This is the way we drink our juice," they all wore smiles again. She finished the song abruptly, praying they would finish their meals in peace.

Eventually, they all turned their attentions back to their food, which gave Shauna a moment to think. She glanced over the group, her gaze finally coming to rest on a chubby little boy.

"Does Bobby Radisson eat all of the time?" Shauna whispered her question, pointing to the rotund toddler who pushed food into his mouth with a vengeance.

"Uh-huh," Ellen mumbled with a nod. "Ever since I started working in the lunchroom, anyway. And it's not just the usual foods. His mother insists on sending him special snacks every day, which the other kids always want. She won't take no for an answer, and neither will he. He has to have them or he cries."

"You're kidding." Out of the corner of her eye, Shauna watched him swallow down his entire meal in less time than most took to say the blessing.

"Nope. I guess on some level the food pacifies him. I'm not sure where the real problem lies, though. Must be something deep down driving the hunger, but I'm not a professional, just a cafeteria worker."

"More, Miss Shauna!" the youngster cried out, as if echoing their thoughts. "I hungry."

She moved in his direction. "But you just finished your lunch," she argued, as she pulled out a paper towel to wipe his sticky hands. "You have to wait until snack time to have more."

He immediately burst into tears, and wailing soon followed.

"Good grief." Shauna looked up at Ellen. "Now what do I do?"

Ellen shrugged and went back to work. Shauna did her best to console the unhappy little boy, but his tears continued on well into the children's nap time, which came right after lunch. In fact, he cried himself to sleep.

Curled up on their mats, the children all eventually dozed off—except Charity, who sang aloud, "Jesus wubs me, dis I know," approximately eight hundred times in a row. Shauna tried to shush her, but the child would not be silenced. Finally, after forty-five minutes of trying to get her to sleep, the weary teacher gave up.

"Let her sing," she mumbled. "Maybe it will wear her out."

It didn't. When the others awoke, Charity was still going strong.

The rest of the afternoon crawled by. Shauna faced one catastrophe after another. Whenever her back was turned, Charity would do something to one of the other children.

"Charity hit me, teacher!"

"Cherry bite me, Miss Shauna!"

"Charity throw blocks, teacher!"

"Cherry, no push! No push!"

"Charity pull hair, teacher."

All afternoon, it continued on. Time and time again, Shauna tried to reason with the little girl, tried to control her without putting her in the time-out corner. But every attempt only led to more anger on the part of the frustrated youngster.

The little darling threw temper tantrums, held her breath, and screamed each and every time something didn't go her way. "I tell my daddy!"

Shauna wasn't sure how many times she heard those words through the course of the day. . .or how many more times she could take hearing them again.

Four o'clock arrived. Time to serve snacks. No sooner were the crackers and juice handed out than Charity began to whine, "Red juice, teacher! Red juice."

"No, Charity. We're drinking apple juice today."

"Red juice!"

They bantered back and forth until Shauna thought she would lose her mind. Finally, she snatched up the cup of juice. "No juice for Charity."

The child burst into tears. "Apple juice, teacher! Apple juice."

Defeated, Shauna placed the cup on the table, where the child willingly took it and began to drink.

Shortly thereafter, Charity began to dance around the room, knocking into toys and tables. "I dance, teacher!" she shouted.

"I see that." Shauna shook her head. "But be careful, honey."

Charity continued to twirl until she spun into Marisa, who burst into tears. Shauna did her best to bring a sense of calm to the room, but her shattered nerves made the task difficult. *Lord, help me make it to the end of this day. Please, Father.*

At 5:00 p.m., many of the parents began to arrive to pick up their children. Lovely Abigail with the long red hair went first, followed by Clay Peterson, the class clown.

Soft-spoken Dinah was next. She embraced Shauna tightly. "My teacher, Mama!" she bragged, as the lovely woman scooped her into her arms.

Joey and Jonathan, the Cameron twins, followed Dinah. Their father traipsed out with one wrapped around his waist, another on his shoulders. Shauna couldn't help but smile.

Mrs. Tarantino came to pick up Marisa, a darling girl who always seemed to have her fingers in her mouth.

She was closely followed by Mr. Chesterfield, a balding man. Shauna had already heard the scuttlebutt about the Chesterfields. Apparently their daughter McKinsey had been a surprise package, delivered when the couple hit their mid- to late-forties. "Bye, Miss Teacher!" she said as she left.

Shauna beamed from ear-to-ear. Why couldn't they all be like that? She glanced across the near-empty room at Charity, who sat in the far corner, playing with a puzzle. Where were her parents? Why weren't they here yet?

Danny left, followed by Elizabeth, the little one who never talked. That left only three—Bobby, April, and Charity.

"You can go now, Shauna," Mrs. Fritz said, entering the room. "These children are usually not picked up until after six, and I always stay with them."

"Are you sure?"

"Of course."

"To be honest, I'd really like to have a few words with Charity's parents," Shauna explained.

"Well, stay if you'd like, but there's something you should know," Mrs. Fritz said, opening her arms wide. Charity ran into her arms, resting her head on the older woman's shoulder.

"How did you do that?" Shauna asked, amazed.

"Do what?"

"How did you—Oh, never mind." She stopped herself

before saying too much. After all, she didn't want her lack of experience to show. "You said there was something I should know?"

"Oh, yes," Mrs. Fritz said, running her fingers through Charity's curls. "This little one doesn't have a m-o-t-h-e-r."

"She doesn't?" That explained so much, but it also raised a host of questions.

"No. So if you need to be speaking to anyone about her, it would be the father or the grandmother. One or the other picks her up—usually the grandmother, Mrs. Dougherty. She runs a bookshop not far from here and is usually one of the last ones to get here each evening."

Shauna stifled a yawn. "Maybe I'll connect with them tomorrow. I really need to get home now."

"I'll see you in the morning, honey," the older woman gave her a gentle pat on the back. "You look like you could stand a long, hot bubble bath and a good book."

"I wish I had that kind of energy," Shauna said with a yawn. More likely, she would hit the bed as soon as she arrived home.

She made her way out to the parking lot, where she climbed into her car for the short drive up I-45. As soon as the key turned in the ignition, unexpected tears trickled down her cheeks.

"I don't know anything about children," she spoke to the empty car. "I'm a total and complete failure." She pulled the car out of the parking lot, hoping none of the parents had seen her outburst. No one must know how wholly inadequate she felt.

☙

"Pastor, I hope you don't mind the intrusion, but I need to talk to someone."

Kent looked up at the young woman in the snug green

dress and slick cherry-red nail polish. *Oh no. Not Vicky Ebert. Not again.*

Mascara cascaded down her flushed cheeks as her words tumbled out with great passion. "I just don't know where else to turn. But I knew I could count on you. Who else can a girl turn to if not her pastor?" She snatched a tissue from her small black handbag and wiped madly.

"Come on in." He glanced at his watch. 5:45 p.m. He needed to get home. He really needed to spend a little time with his daughter before diving into next week's sermon, and yet. . .here stood a wounded parishioner who obviously needed his help. How could he say no to those tears? "Have a seat." He gestured toward the large chair directly across from him. "Please." He left the door ajar, a move he had learned early on when counseling someone of the opposite sex.

"Thank you, Pastor." She took a seat. "I didn't know who else to talk to. I'm just so distraught."

"I can see that. What's happened?"

"Well, you know Josh, right? My ex?" She dabbed at her eyes with the tissue, leaving thick black lines underneath.

"Of course." Kent remembered him well. Josh had struggled with an alcohol problem for the past two years. But he wasn't exactly her "ex." In fact—and Kent knew this firsthand from counseling with Josh—she hadn't even filed for divorce yet.

"He wants me back," Vicky said. "But I don't know what to do. The boys need a father, but not that kind of a father."

That's so odd. I thought he was doing better. "Is he still drinking?"

"He says he's not, but I know he is," she stammered. "I just don't know what to do. I tried to tell him we're not supposed to be together, but he just goes crazy on me."

"What do you mean 'goes crazy'?" Kent asked. "Does he hurt you?"

"Oh no." She blew her nose. "He never hits me."

"The boys? Does he hurt the boys?"

"Not physically." She sighed. "It's not like that. It's just that he gets so loud and demanding. And I don't love him anymore." She dissolved into a puddle of tears. Kent glanced down at his watch once again. 5:47 p.m. "That's a horrible thing to confess, but I feel better now that I've said it. How could I love a monster like that?"

"I don't know, Vicky." Kent's heart began to twist inside him. He ached for Vicky's two little boys. Josh Junior was just four, and Kevin was barely two. They needed a father, but would a loving God really send back the man who had treated Vicky so badly in the past? According to Vicky's description, Josh Ebert seemed to be a hopeless case. Was there no answer to this problem?

"I was so sure he had made steps in the right direction." Kent shook his head, unable to think of anything else to say. "I'm sorry you and the boys are going through this."

"I knew you would be." She looked up at him with sad eyes. "What I need in my life is a man." Her eyes brightened with the idea. "A godly man who will love me and love my little boys like his own."

For a brief second, Kent nodded in sympathy, until he realized her bright blue eyes had locked firmly into his. There was something in her expression that he could not ignore. "Uh, Vicky," he stammered as he stood to his feet, "I think we'd better call it a night. I've got to get home to my daughter and you. . ."

"And I," she reached out to take his hand, "can't thank you enough for being the most awesome pastor a girl could ever have." As she stood, she gave his hand a squeeze. "We are a blessed church. And I feel so much better after talking to you. I knew I would."

"Thank you." Kent pulled away quickly, trying not to hurt her feelings.

"You're always here when I need you. I can't say that about just everyone, you know."

"I have a wonderful idea," he said then reached into his desk drawer. "I have a friend from college—a woman—who is a licensed family therapist. I'm sure she would love to see you. I'll even give her a call if you like."

"But I want to talk to you," Vicky said with a pout. "Not some woman I don't even know. How can she possibly help me? She doesn't even know Josh and the boys, and she certainly wouldn't understand my needs. You've known me for years, going all the way back to tenth-grade geometry class." She gave him a sad puppy-dog face.

Kent looked at his watch once again. 6:08 p.m. "Yes, I do know you." *Better than you think.* "I'd like you to at least think about my suggestion," he said. "Promise?"

"I promise," Vicky flashed a weak smile. "If it will make you happy."

"What makes me happy is irrelevant."

"You're such an important part of our lives," she argued. "And I trust your judgment completely. I really do." She gazed up at him again, her long lashes blinking away the tears.

"Thank you, Vicky." Kent moved toward the door. "But it's the Lord's judgment you should trust, not mine or anyone else's. He has an answer for you and the boys."

"Yes." She reached out to take his hand. "I believe He does."

six

Kent sat at his computer, scrolling through e-mails. He noticed a letter from his sister Jessica in Dallas and opened it immediately. As he read the letter, he couldn't help but whisper a quick, "Praise the Lord." It looked like Jessica and her husband would be able to visit the Houston area during the winter holidays after all. That meant they could participate in the church's Christmas Eve candlelight service.

"I know it's a long time till Christmas," he had written in his most recent e-mail, "but it just won't be the same if you're not here to sing 'O Holy Night.'"

His parishioners would be thrilled and so would his mother. But his daughter, above all, would be filled with joy. She loved her Aunt Jessica and Uncle Colin. And they had played such an important role in her life since Faith's death. Every person who took the time to invest in his daughter's life had become a critical part of the equation.

Kent read over the rest of his e-mails, erasing most. Nothing but advertisements and forwards. Nothing life changing. But speaking of life changing, he had a sermon to write. The pressure to come up with something fresh, something from the heart of God, remained a weekly challenge. He loved this part of ministering—listening for the voice of God and acting on what he heard.

But hearing seemed to be a bit more difficult tonight, for some reason. Perhaps this was due to his ongoing lack of sleep. Or maybe it had something to do with his workload, both at the church and home. Somewhere between caring for a congregation, cooking, washing dishes, doing laundry, and bathing a toddler and tucking her into bed at night, he had worn himself out. At times like these, he truly relied on the Lord to get him through. How else could he possibly take on the role of two parents at once?

His heart grew heavy, as it always did when he allowed his thoughts to shift in this direction. How could he manage without Faith? Then again, he had to confess, he had somehow managed to get through the past two years, day by day, minute by minute. And with the Lord's help, he would go on. Together, he and his beautiful daughter would get through this season of sadness and emerge with faith and hope intact.

Charity chose that very moment to slip behind his chair and startle him with a passionate, "Boo!"

"Boo who?" he echoed as he scooped her up in his arms. He held her close, tickling her tummy, her damp hair still carrying the fresh scent of shampoo. She laughed until her little face turned pink. Kent gave her a tight hug. "I love you, Charity."

"Wub u." She sprang from his lap and raced toward the television. "Movie, Daddy. Movie!" She bounced up and down.

"We can't watch the same movie every single night," he argued as he turned back to his computer screen. "Why don't you be a good girl and play with your toys. It's almost bedtime, anyway."

"Movie, Daddy!"

He sighed deeply, and then stood to grab the all-too-familiar movie case from the bookshelf. "You've seen this hundreds of times," he mumbled, pulling the animated feature from its jacket and slipping it into the DVD player. Within minutes Charity lay curled up on the couch.

Kent sat back down at his computer, trying to concentrate,

but the magical world of toddlerdom kept him distracted from the business at hand. He whispered his thoughts aloud as a prayer, "If you could just give me some idea what to preach on this Sunday, I'd be so happy, Lord. I need You, Lord—not just to help with a sermon, but also to infuse my life. I need your strength. I need Your. . ."

"Cookie, Daddy," Charity reappeared, giving his sleeve a sharp tug.

"It's too late for a cookie, honey," he said. "It's almost bedtime."

"No bed. Movie."

Kent glanced at his watch. "Ten more minutes. That's all."

She scrambled across the room and tossed herself down in front of the large television set. Within moments, she sang along with the familiar animated characters. Kent rubbed his brow and tried to type, but nothing seemed to come.

࿇

Shauna sat at her computer, rubbing her aching brow. *I know you've called me to work with children, Lord, but I don't know how much more of this I can take. I really didn't expect it to be like this. I'm losing my voice. My temper is rising. My head is killing me. And, to top it all off, I think I'm coming down with a cold.* At that, she abruptly sneezed.

With the left-click of the mouse, Shauna signed online, anxious to check her e-mail. Hopefully, Joey had written today. She needed to hear from him. Somehow his words would calm her. They always seemed to.

She thumbed through her e-mail. Junk. Most of it, anyway. Finally, the name and address she had longed to see. *Joey. It's about time.* She anxiously opened the e-mail, taken aback at its brevity.

"Hey, babe," it read, "just wanted to drop you a line to let you know I'm not going to be able to write much. These professors are killing me, and I spend every free minute studying. Hope you understand. I'll try to call sometime next week. I do miss you and hope to see you soon. Let's don't let the distance keep us apart. Love you, babe. Joey."

"That's it? That's what I've been waiting for?"

Her mind reeled as she tried to figure out an appropriate way to respond. Finally, an idea came to her. "I'll mail the letter I printed the other day." She had held onto it for days, not wanting to look pushy. But mailing it the old-fashioned way made perfect sense. He probably just didn't take e-mail seriously enough. A lot of people didn't. She opened the familiar program and entered her letterhead information. "He'll take this seriously," she said. "I hope so, anyway."

She leaned back in the chair, relaxing. She didn't want Joey to think she was overly anxious, but if he didn't take a vested interest in their relationship soon, she would have to have a serious talk with that boy.

As she started to close out the word processor, she stumbled across an unfamiliar file. "What's this?" Her eyes rested on the words, "Living the Dream." *Living the dream?* What in the world. . . ?

She clicked the file open, shocked to see the whole page fill up with sermon notes based on the life of Joseph. "Oh my." *Mr. Twenty-First Century Pastor left this on my computer. I wonder if he needs it. I wonder. . .* She looked the page over, surprised to see how well formulated the notes seemed to be. *And he thinks he's not good at putting his thoughts on paper. Looks pretty good to me.*

She quickly signed back online and added the name "21stcenturypastor" to her Buddy List. His name immediately popped up. "Good. He's still online." Her heart pounded in her ears as she typed. "This is Shauna. We met at the computer store."

"Hey, there," appeared in the box. "I looked for you in church last Sunday. You were a no-show."

"True," she responded. "Sorry about that."

"You missed a great sermon." He followed the comment with a smiley face and Shauna had to chuckle. She could almost see the smile in his eyes.

"Guess I'll have to take your word for it," she typed back. "I went to church with my parents. Their call."

"Understandable," he responded. "So, what's up?"

"I. . ." She paused momentarily as she glanced back over his sermon notes. "I found one of your files on my computer and thought you might need it. I think it's a sermon."

"Great! Can you cut and paste it into an e-mail and send it to me?" he wrote back.

"Yeah. Hang on just a minute." She went back to the word-processing document, highlighting every word of the sermon, then copied it and pasted it into a new e-mail. She typed the address, "*21stcenturypastor@grace.com*." With the click of a button, it was on its way to him.

"Done." She typed in the Instant Message box.

"I can't thank you enough," he wrote back. "I was just sitting here trying to get inspired for next Sunday's sermon."

"You have to get inspired?" she wrote back.

"If I'm not," he responded, "my congregation won't be either. Chances are they'll be snoring in the pew. I can't be responsible for that."

"Sounds like my home church." She couldn't help but smile as she typed the words. "I get a lot of rest on Sundays."

He sent a bright yellow smiley face in response to that. "Maybe you're at the wrong church," he wrote.

"Maybe."

"Well, the invitation still stands. Come for a visit sometime. We've got a lot of programs to offer."

"Programs?" She couldn't help but wonder what he meant.

"We've got a great singles' ministry," he typed back, "and an awesome discipleship program, as well as an inner-city outreach group that helps families in the government housing projects."

"Wow. You must be really busy."

"Yes. In fact. . ." At that, he signed off abruptly.

Shauna leaned back in her chair, thinking about the conversation. "Interesting. Very interesting."

&

Kent stared at the computer monitor as the screen faded to black. "Charity, don't ever do that again!" he scolded. She had deliberately yanked the cord from the wall, turning the computer off while he was in mid-sentence.

"Daddy pway wid me!" she coaxed.

"It's too late to play," he said, scooping her up in his arms. "Time for Charity to go to bed like a good little girl."

"No! Pway, Daddy!" Kent tossed her up in the air, and she squealed in delight. "More, Daddy!" He tossed her again and again, until his arms ached.

"Daddy has to work, baby girl," he said kissing her forehead. "And you have to get some sleep. You've got school tomorrow."

"No school," she pouted as he laid her in the white four-poster bed and pulled covers up to her chin.

"Yes, Charity. You know you have to go to school."

"I work wid you."

"No, honey."

She burst into tears and flung her face in the pillow. "No school, Daddy. Teacher mean."

"Your teacher is mean?" He reached down to stroke her hair. "What did she do to you?"

"She mean, Daddy," Charity said, shaking her head. "No school. No school."

Kent shook his head in disbelief. This was not the first time Charity had complained about the new teacher. Why would Mrs. Fritz hire someone who truly didn't know how to connect with the children? And what should he do about it? *Is it my place?*

As Kent tucked Charity into bed, he struggled with his feelings of frustration. She needed positive influences in her life. She needed her school to be a peaceful, caring place. But these past few days had been particularly difficult on her, and it certainly looked as if the new teacher was to blame.

Looked like the time had come to do something about his daughter's complaints.

seven

"Charity, what are you doing?" Kent looked down at his daughter and shook his head in disbelief. "Where are your clothes?"

The giggling youngster pointed to the floor, where her crumpled Sunday dress lay wadded up next to her shoes and socks. Prancing around in ruffled panties, she chanted merrily. "I no like dress, Daddy! I no like dress!"

"I don't care if you like it or not," Kent said sternly. "You're going to wear that dress to church. Now let's put it back on like a big girl. Daddy's going to be late." He reached down to pick up the delicate dress, holding it carefully. Somehow, just doing so reminded him of Faith. This was one of the few items she had purchased before Charity's birth.

"I know it's silly. The baby's not even here yet. But it was on sale, and I loved it!"

Kent closed his eyes, running his fingers across the lace collar. A loud flush of the toilet brought him back to his senses. "Charity, what are you doing?" He raced into the bathroom just in time to see the water begin to rise to the top of the toilet. A shoe spun madly in the blue water. Two socks, now tinged blue, floated nearby.

"Where is your other shoe?" he demanded, reaching to turn the water off at the wall. He quickly fished the tiny socks out.

"Shoe bye-bye!"

"Charity? What do you mean? Where is your other shoe?"

She pointed at the toilet, erupting into laughter. "I fwush

51

shoe! Shoe bye-bye!" She jumped into the empty bathtub and began to dance about like a banshee. Kent's head drooped to the edge of the toilet seat in frustration.

"Of course you did. Why should this Sunday be different from any other?" He rolled up his sleeve and plunged his arm down into the toilet until he was in almost up to his elbow. His hand finally reached the tiny shoe, which had lodged itself at the base of the toilet. He pulled it out, feeling a momentary surge of triumph. "I got it!" he exclaimed, turning toward Charity. A silent, empty bathtub stared back at him.

He sprang up from the floor and made his way into Charity's bedroom, where he searched, half-frantic, half-frustrated. "Charity!"

"Boo!" She jumped out from behind the door, nearly scaring the wits out of him.

Kent drew in a deep breath and tried to relax. "Charity, come to Daddy. We have to get ready for church." This time she obliged, though he had to bribe her with the promise of a trip to Grandma's house after church in order to accomplish the task.

For the next several minutes, he attempted to balance the task of dressing the precocious youngster, reading over his sermon notes, and searching for his missing Bible. He found it on his bedside table, underneath a picture Charity had colored for him. By the time they reached the church, he felt his nerves had nearly unraveled. With a sigh of relief, he dropped her off in the nursery and headed to his office for a few moments of prayer and reflection.

❧

"What do you mean you're going to another church?" Shauna's mother sat across the breakfast table, looking stunned. "Your father and I were counting on spending the day with you.

We've hardly had a moment with you since you got your new job. And your aunts and uncles will be there. Everyone has missed you."

"I know, Mom," Shauna explained with great care. "But I'm ready for a change. To be perfectly honest, I'm a little bored at your church. There's no one my age there. I had something a little different in mind today."

"Different?" Her mother's eyebrows shot straight up.

"Don't worry," Shauna said with a smile. "I know exactly what I'm doing."

"I sure hope so." Her mother shook her head.

Shauna spent a great deal of time picking out exactly the right outfit. "I look awful in purple," she said, tossing a blouse · onto the bed. "And this gray skirt is too small. I might as well give it away. Hmm. . . What about this?" She held up a soft blue summer dress with short sleeves and a delicate, flowing skirt. "This must be just the ticket. And it's still warm enough to wear a summer dress." She turned around in front of the mirror, holding it up in front of her. "Yes, I do believe so. Mr. Twenty-First Century Pastor is going to be mighty surprised when he sees me in his congregation, I'd be willing to bet."

Shauna's laughter suddenly turned to trembling. She sat slowly on the edge of the bed, realizing just how close she had come to betraying Joey with her thoughts. She cared for him. At least, she was fairly sure she did. Right now, everything seemed a little out of focus.

Lord, show me what to do. I really do need a church where I can feel connected—a part of things. If I'm going just because of Kent Chapman, then stop me in my tracks, Father.

A sense of peace washed over her and she felt, for the first time in a while, like she heard God's heart on the matter. She was in a place where she needed a new church. Nothing wrong in admitting that. She needed people her own age and a good, solid discipleship program.

And her motives weren't off. There was nothing wrong with admiring someone like Kent Chapman simply for being a man of God.

"I'll go," she whispered to no one but herself. "But who knows if I'll even like it."

Sometime later, she found herself in an unfamiliar sanctuary, staring at unfamiliar people. The whole thing felt a little odd, but Shauna determined in her spirit to give the place a fighting chance.

She stood at the back for a while as well-meaning parishioners introduced themselves right and left. An older woman shook hands and offered her a bulletin. A girl about her own age pointed out a "Twenty-Something" class the church was just starting. The worship leader approached her, asking if she might be interested in joining the choir. And when she paused to say hello to a little boy with tight curly hair, his mother—who turned out to be the church's preschool director—asked if she might be interested in working in the nursery.

Right now, to be perfectly honest, Shauna simply wanted to find a place to sit and observe. Perhaps those other things would come in time. She took her place in an empty pew near the back, thankful to be away from the crowd for a moment.

Still, the people came. A beautiful woman with two little boys scooted in next to her. She introduced herself as Vicky Ebert, but not before singing Kent Chapman's praises. Curiosity drove Shauna to glance down at the woman's hand to see if she wore a wedding ring. Nothing. Vicky dove into a lengthy discussion about single parenting, and Shauna tried to focus, but she found it difficult with so much activity going on around her.

An older couple scooted in on her other side. The woman, who introduced herself as Mrs. Witherspoon, filled her in on a program the children's choir would be performing in late October. With great animation, she invited Shauna to attend. Shauna politely nodded and told her she would check her calendar.

Goodness, they're a friendly bunch. Over the past several minutes, Shauna had found herself in comfortable conversation with several folks she had never before met, which served to still her anxious heart. . .until she glanced up at the front of the auditorium and laid eyes on Kent Chapman in his dark gray suit.

Guilt suddenly permeated her being. Why had she come here, after all? To see a man? Had God really drawn her to this place, or were there more evil motives at work?

"I must be crazy," she mumbled, as she looked for the exit at the back of the sanctuary. "Or worse—a heretic." She glanced at her watch, realizing that she probably had just enough time to make it up the aisle and out the door before the opening music began. If she played her cards right, she could be out of here in a flash, and he would never even know she had come. Shauna slipped out—beyond the chattering Vicky Ebert—and into the aisle.

Turning, she immediately found herself face-to-face with Kent Chapman. "Oh, hi. I, uh. . ." *Caught.*

"I'm so happy to see you," the cheerful pastor said with a smile. He extended a hand in her direction. She reached out to shake it, glancing down at his hand.

"What happened to you?" she asked, fighting to hide the laughter in her voice. His white sleeve was covered in tinges of blue.

"Oh, I. . ." He reached to cover it up with his other hand.

"That's a long story. I guess I'll have to tell you later. You weren't leaving were you?"

"Leaving? Me?" Shauna stammered. "Why would I do that? I just got here." She couldn't help but notice the smile that lit his face as she spoke. Her heart suddenly felt warmed by it, though she couldn't explain why. "Could you tell me where the ladies' room is?" she whispered.

He pointed toward the back of the sanctuary and to the left. "It's just around the corner," he whispered back. "But I don't think that's where you were headed. You were going to chicken out on me, weren't you?"

"Chicken out?" she said loudly. "Me? You think I'm scared of your sermons?" She sat defiantly in the pew and reached for her Bible. "You just get on up there and preach, Mr. Twenty-First Century Pastor. I'm all ears.

eight

Shauna gripped the piece of paper in her tightly clenched fist.

"What've you got there, girl?" Ellen asked. "A love letter?"

Shauna tried not to let the frustration show in her voice as she explained. "It is a letter from my boyfriend, but not a love letter. He's supposed to be coming down to meet my parents sometime soon, but. . ."

"But what?" Ellen almost dropped the large jar of jelly.

"He's going on a weekend fishing trip with some of his buddies. Which is okay, of course, but I really hoped he would come to see me sometime before the end of the month. Now it looks like I'll have to wait till the end of October when he has his fall break." She sighed, not knowing if she could take being away from him another month.

"So, are you two an item?" Ellen asked, licking grape jelly off of her fingers. "I mean, are you getting engaged?"

Shauna shrugged, folding the paper and putting it in her pocket. "I'm clueless," she said with a shrug. "If you had asked me that a couple of months ago, I might have said yes, but nothing is clear right now. Nothing but being here and working and spending time with my family."

"Who needs guys anyway?" Ellen said with a smirk. "They only break your heart."

"Aw, come on," Shauna said, "Let's stop talking about them. Besides, I need to get back to the kids." She pointed to the table where the children sat eating ice cream.

"It's unusually quiet today," Ellen observed, looking at the group. "What's up?"

"Charity's not here."

"Ah."

"She's got a stomachache," Shauna explained. "Her grandmother called this morning to say she wasn't coming in today, so I decided to throw myself a little party." She held up her bowl of ice cream.

Ellen screwed the top back onto the jar of jelly. "You're cruel."

"No, I'm not," Shauna argued. "I've only worked here two weeks, and I'm already thinking about quitting."

"You're not."

"I am. You should try working with that kid. She's completely impossible. Do you know what she did the other day?"

"No telling."

"She went to the bathroom then smeared it all over the wall."

"Yuck!"

"Yeah, no kidding. And guess who got to clean it up. But that wasn't all. Remember the other day when the kids were watching *The Lion King*?"

"Yeah."

"I must have gotten a little too wrapped up in the movie," Shauna said with a shrug, " 'cause the next thing I know, she's in my purse, getting out my lipstick."

"You're kidding."

"I wish I were. She covered half of her face before I could snatch it out of her hands. Then she broke it. My best lipstick."

"I'm so sorry, Shauna." Ellen reached out to place a hand on her shoulder. "It seems like you've had nothing but trouble with that little girl."

"I know this is terrible," Shauna said with a slight groan,

"but I'm praying her family will move her to another school. Is that awful? I know it's awful, but I'm ready to quit over one little girl." Her words came fast and furiously. "Is it really possible for one child to so completely disrupt my life?"

"It's possible. Obviously."

"Well, I know this sounds just terrible, but I don't know how much more of it I can take. Sometimes I think I learned absolutely nothing in school. I should be able to handle things like this. I really should." Shauna shook her head in defeat. "I feel so helpless sometimes."

"Just give it time," Ellen responded. "You're still on a learning curve."

"Looks like I will be for a long, long time."

"In the meantime, looks like you've got another problem on your hands." Ellen pointed to the table, where three of the children had started putting ice cream in one another's hair.

"Great." Shauna shook her head in despair. "I tell you—some days I just want to go back to school and get my beautician's license."

❧

Kent yawned loudly and leaned back in his oversized chair. Pictures of Shauna Alexander in that blue dress wouldn't seem to leave him. "Snap out of it, man. You've got a lot of work to do." He turned back toward the pile of mail that needed to be answered.

Another yawn erupted, a reminder of his lack of sleep. Charity had cried late into the night, refusing to settle down in her own bed. Frustrated, he had relented, allowing her to crawl into bed next to him. That didn't work either. She was too fussy to rest. His solution had come in the form of a car ride at 2:15 a.m. The movement had lulled her to sleep. Exhausted, he had tumbled into bed sometime around 3:00 a.m.

He was awakened at 5:30 a.m., when Charity insisted it was time to begin the day. No sooner did he get her dressed than she lost the contents of her breakfast all over the living room carpet. Instead of spending the day at the day care, she would stay with his mother, who, thank goodness, happened to be taking a day off from the bookstore.

Kent felt particularly guilty leaving her on a day like today when she didn't feel well. He tried to balance that guilt against the exhaustion that so often permeated him these days. Would it continue forever? He stifled back a yawn, trying to focus. With so much to be done, he must remain clearheaded. There were e-mails to be sent, sermons to be written, phone calls to be made.

Phone calls. He needed to go over the visitor list from last Sunday and make the usual calls to thank them for their visit. It was a logical thing to do. Nothing out of the ordinary there. Yes, there were phone calls to make. And he suddenly knew which visitor he would call first.

Kent punched in the number with a bit of anxiety. The phone rang one, two, three times. On the fourth ring an answering machine kicked in. "You've reached the Alexanders. We're not here to take your call right now, but if you leave a message, we'll get back to you. Have a blessed day."

Kent fumbled for words, preparing to give his rehearsed speech. Funny, once he started talking, everything seemed to come out backwards, upside-down. He couldn't even manage to speak in a simple sentence. He struggled to get his message across, to ask that all-important question. When he felt that there was nothing left to say, he hung up, dejected.

"Great. She'll think I'm nuts."

࿇

Shauna listened to the messages, hoping to hear Joey's voice.

At the very least, he owed her a phone call. Then again, he hadn't called once since her arrival in Houston. Most of the messages were for her mother or father. She was just about to give up entirely when an oddly familiar voice kicked in. Was that. . .? Nah, it couldn't be.

"Shauna, this is Pastor Chapman. I mean, Kent Chapman. First of all, thank you for coming last Sunday. I hope you enjoyed the service. We enjoyed having you. I. . ." He seemed to hesitate a bit here, and she wondered where he might be headed. "I, uh. . .I enjoyed seeing you again. In fact. . ." His voice broke again. "I was wondering if you were free this Friday night. I thought maybe dinner and a movie might be nice. I know this is a little, well. . . I know we hardly know each other, but. . ."

There was a definitive pause in the message. Shauna smiled as his voice kicked in again. "Okay, this is it. . . . I'd love to see you this Friday night. Call me at the church if you're even remotely interested. The number is in the bulletin you got on Sunday. Or call me at home. Unless you think this is completely inappropriate. But. . ." His voice trailed off. "I really prayed before calling, I promise. I never do things like this. Never."

Shauna tried to imagine the expression on his face as he left the message—the obvious fear in those beautiful green eyes. Was he worried, nervous? He certainly sounded like a teenager asking a girl out for the first time.

And she felt a bit like a teenager right now, as well. A date? How did she feel about that? Shauna bit her lip nervously. Should she call him back? Would that be inappropriate? After only a moment's pause for reflection, she picked up the phone to return Kent Chapman's call.

nine

"How do I look?" Kent asked, turning for inspection.

"Handsome, as always," his mother responded with a smile. "Would you expect me to say anything else?"

He shrugged then fumbled to straighten his collar. "Do you think it's too much? We're just going out to dinner."

"You look fine, Kenny," she insisted.

"Mom, don't call me. . ." He hesitated before finishing the sentence. After so many years on the job, she should be free to call him whatever she liked.

"I know, *Kent*," she said, emphasizing his name. "But sometimes I forget, that's all."

"Nana!" Charity said, tugging at her grandmother's skirt. "Watch TV."

"Yes, darling." She swept the youngster up into her arms. "As soon as Daddy goes, we'll watch a video together. Now give him a good-bye kiss."

Kent reached over to embrace his daughter. Spoiled or not, she remained his jewel. For a brief moment, he felt sure he saw Faith in her twinkling eyes.

His mother gave Charity a gentle kiss on the cheek. "I picked up a little gift for our girl yesterday. . ." She reached into a bag and came out with a baby doll. "She's so pretty. See?" She straightened the doll's skirt before placing her into the youngster's waiting arms.

"You're going to spoil her," Kent warned, though he knew his words fell on deaf ears.

"Pshaw!"

"See you no later than ten," he said.

His mother signaled for Charity. "Tell Daddy good-bye, honey," she instructed.

Charity managed a joyous "Bye-bye" before turning her attentions toward the television.

Kent planted a kiss on his beautiful daughter's cheek. "Bye, baby." He turned to his mother and mouthed the words, "I can't thank you enough."

"Oh, pooh!" she answered. "I love watching her. You know that. Besides, we've wanted to get you married off for quite some time now."

"Mom, don't. . ."

"Get on out of here," she said with a grin. "And have a good evening. Don't give us a second thought."

⋆

Shauna slipped on the blue floral dress and gazed at her reflection in the mirror. "What do you think, Mom?"

Her mother nodded her approval. "Nice, babe. But you still haven't told me anything your young man."

"He's not my young man," Shauna said nervously, pulling the dress off and reaching for a brown skirt. "He's just someone I met at the computer store."

"What's his name?"

"Kent Chapman."

"What does he do for a living?"

Shauna paused only slightly as she zipped up the skirt. "He's a pastor."

"A pastor? Really." Her mother's eyes widened with amazement. "That would explain last Sunday."

"Yes, but please don't say anything." Shauna reached for a beige blouse. "At least not yet. I barely know him."

"You must want to get to know him," her mother said with a smile, "or you wouldn't be so worried about what you're wearing."

Shauna hurried to button up her blouse. "I'm not worried, Mom."

"Really? Then why have you buttoned your blouse like that?"

Shauna looked down, horrified to find the buttons and buttonholes mismatched. "Good grief." As she fumbled to straighten out the mess, she could sense her mother's gaze. "Just say it, Mom."

"Say what?"

"You're wondering about Joey. You're thinking I have no right to be going out with someone I barely know when Joey is supposed to be my boyfriend."

"Actually, I wasn't thinking that at all," her mother said. "And I've never even met Joey, remember? I'm just an incurable romantic, and I want the best for you. This fella could very well be the one."

"You? An incurable romantic?" Shauna laughed in spite of herself.

"Yes," her mother said, her expression serious. "Whether you want to believe it or not. Now tell me more about this pastor. How old is he?"

"I don't know. Late twenties, probably."

"Wow. That's young. What does he look like?"

For some reason, all Shauna could see were his dancing green eyes. She felt her lips curl up in a satisfied grin. "Very nice looking. But you'll find that out for yourself any minute now. He should be here soon." Shauna glanced in the mirror and groaned. "Could you hand me the hairbrush? My hair looks ridiculous."

"You look great." Her mother smiled as she reached to offer her assistance.

"Thanks, Mom."

The doorbell rang suddenly, startling Shauna. "Oh, dear." She gave herself one last glance in the mirror. "My hair looks terrible. I wanted to put it up."

"It looks better down," her mother assured her. "Now, do you want to get the door, or should I?"

"Um. I don't know," she said nervously. "I don't want to look too anxious. Why don't you get it?"

Just then her father's booming voice rang out, "Shauna, your young man is here."

She groaned loudly. "Great. Daddy got to him first." She knew how intimidating her father could be. A retired navy captain, he was quite large in stature and had a deep, booming voice. He was a teddy bear at heart, but people who didn't know him well often misunderstood his sense of humor. Shauna was halfway to the living room when she heard her father's voice ring out again.

"Come in here, young fella," he said sternly. "Nothing to be afraid of. We won't bite."

Shauna flinched, trying to imagine what Kent must be thinking. She rounded the corner, nearly bumping into him. "Oh. So sorry," she said, glancing up. He looked incredible in his dark gray button-up shirt and black slacks. She couldn't help but notice the subtle but intoxicating scent of cologne.

"You look really nice, Shauna," Kent said, his gaze resting on her hair.

"Thank you," she mumbled, embarrassed. "I, uh, I'd like to introduce you to my mother and father—Max and Gloria Alexander. Mom, Dad. . .this is Kent Chapman."

Her father extended his hand, grasping Kent's tightly.

From the pained expression on Kent's face, perhaps a bit too tightly.

"Glad to meet you, son," her father said, slapping him on the back. "Any friend of Shauna's is a friend of ours."

"Shauna tells us you're a pastor," her mother said, looking at him curiously. "If you don't mind my asking. . ."

Shauna grimaced. *Oh, please don't give him the third degree, Mother.*

"I was just wondering what prompted you to go into the ministry."

Kent quickly shared the story, and she seemed more than satisfied with his explanation. "Sounds like a big job for someone so young, but you have a lot of passion."

"Thank you. Sometimes I think I have too much passion—but the need is so great."

"You're sure right about that," Shauna's father threw in. "I'm proud of you, young man. But what's the name of your church? Maybe I've heard of it."

"Grace Community Church. We're not too far from downtown, just east of I-45."

"Why, Grace Community!" Shauna's mother said with a smile. "Isn't that the church I hear so much about—the one that's always doing those big outreaches in the community—giving away food and all of that?"

"Yes, ma'am. Probably, anyway. There are so many churches in the Houston area reaching out to the community. We're just one of them. But happy to be serving so near the heart of the city. It's certainly worth the drive."

Shauna watched him carefully as he spoke. She couldn't help but notice the gleam in his eyes as he talked about the church. Clearly, he loved his job.

"Well," she said, glancing at her watch, "we're going to have to get going." She reached up and gave her mother a peck on the cheek.

"Don't stay out too late, you two," her father said sternly.

"He's kidding," Shauna whispered to Kent as they made their way out the door.

"I know," he whispered back. "But I like it. I think he's great."

She smiled, as she pondered his comments. What a good heart he had. Why couldn't Joey be more like this? Why couldn't he. . .

No. I won't think about him tonight. Tonight, Joey doesn't exist. And even if he did exist, he couldn't begin to measure up to what's standing directly in front of me.

ten

Shauna smiled at Kent as he pulled the door of the restaurant open. From inside, the aroma of garlic and spice greeted her.

"I love Italian food," she said with a grin.

"I know."

"How did you know?" She stared at him curiously.

"I had your computer, remember?" he said with a smile. "I learned a few things about you. Macaroni Grill is your favorite restaurant, right?"

"Okay, stop right there," she said, putting her hand up to squelch any further conversation on the matter. "I don't want to know anything else you might have read on my computer."

"I'm just kidding," he said with a grin. "I asked your dad where I should take you, and he suggested Italian food. Said you had loved it since you were a little girl."

"You talked to my dad? When?"

"I called him this morning from the church. He's a great guy. Shared all sorts of information about you and told me a little about himself, as well. He has quite a past."

"Yes, he does." Shauna smiled up into Kent's kind eyes before finally speaking her mind. "Are you always this nice?"

"I try hard not to be. It's bad for my image, you know." He laughed, and she joined him.

Together, the pair made their way up to the hostess. "Two for non-smoking," Kent said.

The hostess grabbed her pen. "Name please."

"Chapman."

"It's going to be about a fifteen-minute wait." Her curt voice had an edge of exhaustion to it. Shauna wondered how Kent would respond.

"That's fine," he said with no stress to be noted in his voice, "Take your time. We're in no hurry."

Shauna looked around for a place to sit. "Looks like we might have to wait outside," she said. "I think I saw some benches out front." Her heart skipped a beat as Kent opened the door and waited for her to step through. *He's such a gentleman.* She smiled in his direction as they approached the bench together. He waited until she was seated before sitting.

Shauna looked up as she heard children's voices. Off in the distance, a youngster, probably four or five, swung on a wrought-iron railing near the restaurant door.

"Some people just let their kids do anything and get away with it," she said, pointing. "Do you see that?"

"Yeah. He's a cute kid."

"Yes, but do you see what he's doing? He could get hurt. And look at his mother—just standing there, ignoring him. Doing nothing. I tell you, nothing frustrates me more than parents who won't control their children."

Kent's lips tightened before he spoke. When he did, his words surprised her. "Being a parent isn't easy. Before my daughter was born, I felt the same way you do now. But, I'm telling you, it's nearly impossible to keep up with a toddler. I, uh, I have a daughter, you know. Not sure if you caught that on Sunday. She was in the nursery."

"What?" Shauna tried to make sense of his shocking comment but found herself too stunned to comprehend clearly. "I don't understand. Are you divorced?" Her mind reeled. *He can't be divorced. He's a pastor. On the other hand, he did say he had a past. I can't assume.*

"No," Kent's eyes shifted to the ground. "I lost my wife two and a half years ago. She. . ." His eyes grew misty, and he swallowed hard. "She was killed in a car accident on Interstate 10. Hit by a drunk driver on her way home from a Bible study. It was her first night out with her girlfriends after having the baby."

Shauna gasped. "I'm so sorry."

"There's no reason for you to be," he said tenderly. "I've gotten over the most painful part. Time has a way of healing much of the hurt. But every time I look into my little girl's face, I'm reminded again of Faith."

"Faith. That's a beautiful name."

"For a beautiful lady," he said wistfully.

"What's your daughter's name?" Shauna asked, gazing at him with newfound admiration and curiosity.

"Oh, her name is. . ."

"Chapman!" A voice over the loudspeaker rang out his name suddenly, startling them both. "Chapman, table for two."

He laughed, half startled at the interruption. "Guess we'd better get inside before they give our table away. We can finish this conversation later."

❧

Kent pulled the chair out, eyes following Shauna's every move. She sat carefully, placing her handbag on the floor next to the chair.

"So, how's your computer?" he asked, trying to make light conversation.

"Fine. And yours?"

"Fine." He looked at her with a smile, relaxing. "I don't know why I'm so nervous. Then again, I, uh, I haven't been on a date since my wife passed away. But listen. . .let's change the conversation. I want to know about you. Tell me everything."

"Everything?"

"Yes. Start at the beginning. Where are you from? Your parents seem really nice. Very loving. Do you have brothers and sisters?"

"I'm an only child," she explained. "And spoiled rotten."

"I know how that goes," he said, thinking of Charity. "I'm not sure how a parent is supposed to act with an only child. Ever since Faith died. . ." He stopped himself quickly. "I'm sorry. I did it again."

"That's okay," Shauna said with a smile. "You can talk about her if you like. It won't hurt my feelings."

Kent shook his head. "No. This is a new day. I know that God has already given me all the comfort I could ever need. He's been with me all the way. I don't know why things happen like they do sometimes, but after more than two years of agonizing over everything that has happened, I can honestly say He never gives us more than we can bear."

"I know that's right." Shauna said with a nod. "I haven't been through anything like you, but I lost my grandparents at a young age. My mom's parents, that is. They were killed in a house fire when I was seven. We were very close, and losing them almost killed me."

"I'm so sorry." He paused for a moment. "My grandmother passed away a few years ago. She was a big part of our family. My grandpa Buck is the only living grandparent I've got, but he's in a retirement home. I need to see him more."

They looked at each other in silence for a moment before Shauna shifted the conversation a bit. Kent was grateful for the change in subject.

Shauna's face contorted as she spoke. "Speaking of things that are hard to deal with, I guess I should tell you a little bit about my job. Don't know if this is the best time because I feel like I'm in over my head right now."

"Really? What's going on?"

"It's just that I feel like such a failure. I spent all of those years in school learning everything I could about kids, and now I feel like I know nothing at all."

"Just wait till you're a parent," Kent said with a laugh. "You find out that you know absolutely nothing. Nothing at all. But you never finished telling me about yourself. You're an only child. How long have you lived in Houston?"

"Oh, forever," she exclaimed. "I'm a Texan, born and bred. What about you?"

"I was born here in Houston," he shared. "Lived on the north end all of my life. A suburban kid. Everything about my life was fairly typical until I hit my teens. That's when my father passed away."

"Oh, I'm so sorry." Her eyes reflected genuine sympathy.

"It was awful," he acknowledged. "And unfortunately, I let the incident drive me to do the wrong things. I turned to my friends for support, and they were more than willing to show me their way of coping with the pain."

"What do you mean?"

"I got involved with drinking and drugs. I. . ." his gazed shifted to the table. "The whole thing was awful. But everything came to a head when I was involved in a car accident that almost killed one of my friends. I was hurt pretty bad myself."

"Oh, Kent. . ."

"I wasn't driving," he was quick to add, "but I might as well have been. We all lived so close to the edge that it could have been any one of us at any time. And when you're hurting like I was, you just want the pain to end. I guess in some way, I probably wanted to die back then."

"Wow."

"You'd think the accident would have been enough to set me on the right course, but I didn't give up some of my bad habits until my mom remarried. My stepdad is great. And I didn't realize how much I needed a male role model until he came into the picture. God began to work on my heart about that same time."

"You've been through so much."

"Yeah." He shrugged. "I guess you could say I have a 'testimony,' but I still tell the kids in the youth group that the greatest testimony of all is living a life for God—uninterrupted by the junk of this world."

"Agreed." She smiled warmly. "I guess you could say I have that kind of testimony. I'm one of those kids who was raised in church and loved the Lord from the time I was a little girl. Never really got involved in drugs or anything like that."

"That's wonderful." Kent gave her an admiring look. "And that's exactly what I want for my daughter." He paused for a moment before asking, "Did you enjoy growing up in the Houston area?"

Shauna laughed. "Yeah. I loved it here as a kid. My parents were big on horseback riding and the rodeo. What about you? Your family into the whole country/western scene like most everyone else around here?"

"Hardly," he said with a laugh. "My parents were into the opera, the symphony. The arts, in general. My sister Jessica sings with the Dallas Metropolitan Opera."

"Wow." Shauna gave him a wide-eyed stare. "That's amazing. I can't sing a note."

"I sing a little," he said with a shrug. "And play the guitar. Just enough to occasionally lead worship in the youth group."

"You're a man of many talents."

"I love good music," he explained. "And going to the theater—that kind of thing. But now that I've got my daughter to think of things are changing a little. Her idea of entertainment is an evening at Chuck E. Cheese's followed by a cartoon video. Things are shifting pretty rapidly around our place."

"I know what you mean," Shauna agreed. "Ever since I took my job—" She stopped herself abruptly. "No, I won't talk about that. I'm not at work right now, and I made myself a promise I would try to put this day behind me. Trust me, if you had any idea what sort of week I'd had, you'd understand."

"Oh, I understand all right," he concurred. "Trust me. I understand."

❧

Shauna walked up to the front door, nervously anticipating her last moments alone with Kent.

"I had a great time," she said, coming to a stop just under the porch light.

He grinned then shifted his gaze to the ground. "Me, too. Not bad for a first date."

"Not bad at all." She reached into her purse for a house key. She fumbled for a minute or two, finally giving up. "I must have left my key inside," she said, reaching to ring the bell.

Kent caught her hand just before she touched it. "Wait. I mean, do you mind waiting just a minute?"

"Of course not," she said, turning back toward him, her heart beginning to race. *If he tries to kiss me on our first date, it will ruin everything.*

"I just wanted to say thank you," Kent said, taking hold of her hand. Shauna began to tremble immediately. "The last few weeks I feel like all I ever do is rush back and forth between home and the church. Taking care of a toddler is so hard, and work isn't much easier. But tonight has been great."

"For me, too," Shauna said, giving his hand a squeeze.

"What I'm trying to get at is. . ." He looked nervous. Very nervous. "Would you like to do this again sometime?"

Shauna looked at the anxious young man before her. *How could I turn that down, Lord?* "I'd love to," she said. And then, for some reason completely unknown to her, Shauna reached up and gave him a gentle kiss on the cheek.

eleven

Kent yawned then glanced at the clock on his desk. 11:47 a.m. "Feels like the day should already be over." He hadn't slept much last night. In fact, most of the hours had whittled away while he argued with Charity about sleeping in her own bed. He had lost the fight—as usual.

"Lord, she's getting harder to control every day. I don't know what I'm going to do with her. I know she's spoiled, but. . ."

Kent just couldn't seem to finish the sentence. He didn't have an answer, and though he prayed about the situation daily, things only seemed to be getting worse.

She needs her mother.

The words raced through his mind before he could stop them. Unexpected tears followed. Kent laid his head on his desk and wept openly. *I miss Faith so much. She would have been such a wonderful mother to Charity. I can't do this by myself, Lord.*

Warm tears rolled down his cheeks, but he pushed them away as he drew in a deep breath and tried to gain control of his senses. His daughter needed the influence of a godly woman—someone who could show her how to grow into the woman of God she was destined to become. Charity would never know her mother, but perhaps the Lord would bring the right woman in her life—to mentor and to love.

Shauna Alexander. For some reason, Kent couldn't help but think of her. *She loves children. She said so herself. And she's trained to work with them. Is that what You're doing here, Lord? Have You brought Shauna into my life so that Charity will have her influence?* Or had the Almighty brought Shauna Alexander into his life to satisfy the empty ache in his own heart that seemed to consume him each day since Faith's death?

Once again, the tears came, though slightly softer now. Would he betray Faith if he began to care for someone else? He reached up to touch the spot on his cheek where Shauna had softly kissed him just a few short nights ago. Shauna clearly felt something that night, too. There was no denying the physical attraction, but Kent knew he had to move carefully—to protect both his own heart and that of his daughter.

There was so much at stake this time around. "But Lord, I leave it in Your hands. You know what Charity and I need even better than I do, that's for sure."

A light tap on the office door roused him. He lifted his head and wiped his eyes. His secretary, Joanna, stuck her head inside, looking at him curiously. "You've got a visitor," she said with a smile. His mother made her way through the door.

"Mom." His fears automatically vanished. Even at his age, being around his mother always made things better.

"Are you all right?" she asked as she crossed the room toward him.

"I am now. I was just having a—a moment."

She nodded sympathetically. "You deserve those moments, Kent. Healing takes time. Lots of time." She sat in the chair across from his desk, gesturing for him to have a seat, as well.

He shrugged as he sat. "Sometimes I just get so worried about Charity."

"Something wrong with our girl?"

"No, nothing specific," he explained. "It's just that she gets harder to control every day, and I'm not doing the best job in the world at disciplining."

"Even with two parents in the household, you'd still face that problem," his mother assured him. "Trust me, I know. Would you like me to remind you of what you were like at her age?"

Kent groaned. "I've heard all the stories. Don't think we need to go through that again."

"This is a stage she's going through, Kent. It's called the 'Terrible Twos.'"

"That's what you said last year," he responded with a groan, "and things have only gotten worse. She's almost three, remember?"

"I never said it ended at three!" His mother raised her hands in self-defense. "Some children take years to get through this stage of development. In fact, if memory serves me correctly, I struggled with you until you were nearly four. And then there were the teen years. Remember those?"

Kent leaned his head down onto his desk again. "I don't know how you did it."

"A lot of prayer and some good sensible discipline." She gave him a knowing look. "And if anyone knows what it's like to go it alone—without the help of a spouse—I do. In the years after your father died. . ."

Her eyes misted over, and Kent pressed a tissue into her palm. "In the years after your father died, I felt like a part of me died, too," she said. "I have to confess, I let you get away with far too much in those first couple of years because I was just so absorbed with my own grief, I couldn't cope with much more."

"I remember." Kent knew all too well what he had gotten away with during those critical years.

"If not for the Lord, I doubt I would have survived," his mother explained. "But I did more than survive, honey." She reached to touch his hand. "I'd like to think I'm an overcomer. I'm in a new place now, as are you. You still have a future ahead of you and so does Charity."

"I just worry that I can't do this alone."

"You're not alone. It might feel like it sometimes, but you're not. And just so you know—Charity might be a challenge right now, but she's going to grow into a beautiful young woman whom we'll all be extremely proud of."

He managed a smile with his response, "In the meantime, I'm sure not getting much sleep."

She snickered. "You should be used to that by now."

"I'm not. In fact, if you and Andrew didn't live so close, I don't know what I would have done. You've been such a big help to me. I can never pay you back."

"Pooh." She said with a smile. "That's what grandparents do. But that reminds me why I stopped by. I'm headed out of town tonight for that women's retreat. Did you remember? You'll have to pick up Charity from day care tonight."

"Oh, man." Kent flipped through his memo pads, looking for a familiar one. "I've got an appointment at five thirty with the folks from the Houston Food Bank to discuss the Thanksgiving Outreach. I can't get out of it."

"Well, you'll have to work something out," she said, glancing nervously at her watch, "because I'm on my way right now. In fact, the other ladies are already in the church van waiting on me."

Kent bit his lip as he stood to give her a hug. "Have a good time, Mom. And don't worry. It's under control."

"Sure it is." She responded with a grin then turned toward the door.

ಸ

"Well?" Ellen asked, staring at Shauna. "How did it go?"

"Great," she said, trying not to show too much excitement. "He's such a nice guy—a real gentleman. But I found out something kind of odd. He has a child."

"You're kidding."

"No. But she sounds really sweet—a little precocious, maybe."

"What's her name?"

"Charity!" Shauna called out frantically as the youngster hit Dinah on the head with a spoon. "We don't hit."

"I no hit her, teacher," Charity said with a pout. "She hit me."

Shauna walked over to her, taking the spoon from the child's hand. "Charity can sit in time-out again until she learns to tell the truth."

"No, teacher!" The little girl began to cry in earnest. "I sorry I hit. I sorry!"

Shauna shook her head in disbelief and reached to take the youngster by the hand. "That's fine, Charity, but you've still got to sit in time-out. Now come with me."

Charity kicked and screamed all the way across the room, but sat obediently in the corner at Shauna's leading. *At least we're making some progress.* "Now sit still until the others are finished," she instructed. She made her way back to the table to see about the others. Little Dinah had dried her eyes and turned her attention to Abigail, who clutched an item of her mother's clothing, left for that very purpose. *What am I going to do about that? This has turned into an everyday obsession.*

"I have to go potty, teacher." Clay Peterson bounced up and down.

"We're almost finished with lunch, honey," she said. "Can you wait?"

"Now, teacher!"

"All right," she instructed, pointing just a few yards away to the bathroom door. "But come right back."

He nodded with a sly grin and then shot across the room.

"What were you saying?" Ellen asked, as Shauna turned her attentions back to the conversation once again.

"Oh, I was saying Kent has a daughter," she said. "But I didn't get her name. I think we must have gotten distracted."

At that point, Charity began to wail loudly from the corner. "I want my daddy. I want my daddy!"

Shauna sighed deeply and leaned against the counter. "Now what do I do?"

"Look on the bright side," Ellen scraped leftover food into the garbage disposal. "The day's almost over. You've only got five and a half hours left."

"Right."

Just as Shauna took a step in Charity's direction, a five-year-old boy ran from the bathroom hollering, "Clay pee-peed in the trash can. Clay pee-peed in the trash can."

Shauna slapped herself in the head. Ironically, the only person she hurt was herself. She headed off to the restroom to deal with the prankster, hoping the rest of the day would flow a bit more smoothly.

Throughout the afternoon she struggled with how she felt about Charity. Clearly, the child needed discipline, not just at school but also in her own home. Her situation warranted some sympathy, to be sure, but not this much.

Shauna must work up the courage to speak to Charity's family about her behavior. Surely this was the only answer. Together they would come up with a workable plan to get the little girl through this difficult season.

She spent the better part of the afternoon writing the speech in her head. By the time the workday came to a close, the message had been crafted in its entirety. Shauna stayed behind after most of the other children left, preparing herself for the inevitable. Mrs. Fritz startled her by entering the room at 6:25 p.m.

"Shauna, what are you still doing here?" The older woman

glanced at her watch then looked up at Shauna with curiosity. "It's nearly six thirty."

"I know." Shauna continued to put toys away as she spoke. "I've decided to stay a little later tonight. I'm going to wait until someone comes to pick up you-know-who so that we can have a little talk about her behavior."

"You-know-who?" Mrs. Fritz looked around until her gaze fell on the youngster in the corner. "You mean Charity? What's she done?"

"What hasn't she done?" Shauna continued to pick up toys as she spoke. "She flushed my contact case down the toilet. How she got it, I have no idea. She bit Dinah. I documented that, just in case the parents had any questions. She refuses to obey. No matter what I tell her to do, she won't do it." Shauna looked to the director for a sympathetic smile, but did not receive one. Instead, Mrs. Fritz's face remained taut with concern.

"That's so odd." The director gazed at the youngster compassionately. "I never seem to have that sort of trouble with her."

Shauna bit her lip to keep from responding. "Well," she said finally, "I've had nothing but trouble with her, and I really feel I need to tell them so. Discipline needs to begin at home, so I'll be looking to them for serious help on the home front."

The day-care director's brow furrowed a bit. "Just promise me you'll choose your words carefully."

"Of course I will."

"Things aren't always what they appear to be," Mrs. Fritz continued, "so be careful not to overreact."

"I won't."

Shauna took Charity by the hand, and together they walked up the hallway to the front door. There they waited, Shauna biting her nails and Charity coloring a picture.

Shauna looked at the large clock on the wall. 6:35 p.m. *They're late. Don't they know the center closes at six thirty?*

Shauna continued to wait, looking through the glass front door into the large parking lot. A familiar vehicle pulled up, causing her heart to skip a beat. When Kent Chapman stepped out of the car, she found herself in a semi-hypnotic state. *What in the world? Well, this is a pleasant distraction.*

Shauna opened the front door, letting him in. "I don't believe it," she said with a cool grin. "How did you figure out where I worked?"

"Where you work?" He looked confused.

"How did you find me?" She couldn't help but wonder, though the fact that he would take the time to find her workplace warmed her heart.

The puzzled look never left his face. "Find you?"

"Yeah. How did you know which day-care center to look for?"

"Shauna, I. . ."

"You could have just called," she whispered, looking around for Mrs. Fritz. "Not that I'm not happy to see you. I am. I really am. But our director's not really keen on strangers coming into the facility. Just the parents."

He had a curious look on his face, one she could not seem to read. For some reason, he looked nearly as surprised to see her as she did to see him. Something about all of this just seemed. . . wrong. Off.

"Shauna, you—you don't understand," Kent stammered.

"What do you mean?"

"I mean. . ." He reached out his arms to scoop up an all-too-familiar youngster. "I *am* a parent. And I'm here to pick up my daughter. That's all. To be honest, I didn't have a clue you worked here."

Shauna stared in disbelief at the child in his arms and fought to catch her breath. *You've got to be kidding me.*

"Charity?"

❧

Kent drove home in numbed silence, trying to absorb Shauna's words. *Your daughter needs discipline. You daughter is a problem in the classroom. Your daughter. . .*

How could Shauna Alexander possibly begin to understand all that his daughter meant to him? How could she comprehend the fact that Charity was the last piece of Faith he had—the only lasting reminder? How dare she spend so much time focusing on the negative without once mentioning Charity's need for love and acceptance?

In her entire conversation, she hadn't taken the time to once address the need in Charity's life, only the lack. Well, he would show her. He would telephone Mrs. Fritz and deal with this first thing in the morning.

Just as soon as he had a chance to cool down and think a little more rationally.

"Daddy?" Charity's voice rang out. He heard it, but his thoughts wouldn't still themselves long enough to respond. Shauna had no right to pass judgment on a child she barely knew. She had only worked at the school a few weeks. And Mrs. Fritz would have let him know if Charity was really as bad as all that.

"Daddy!" Charity let out another squeal. "Teacher mean!"
Yes, she is.

"Teacher mean. Charity no like teacher."

"I know, honey." He sighed. "But don't worry about that now. We're going home."

"Go store." She kicked her feet against the back of his seat.

"No. We're going home, honey, not the store."

"Go store, Daddy. Buy baby a toy." Whining followed then a few tears.

"You're not a baby anymore," he corrected. "You're Daddy's big girl."

"Toy!"

"We're going home, Charity."

She let out a cry, and he struggled to keep his wits about him as he drove. Sure, Charity was a handful, but so were all two- and three-year-olds. No reason to think she surpassed the other children with bad behavior.

"Toy, Daddy!" Charity continued to cry out. "We go to store!"

"No store, Charity. Now be a good girl and stop crying."

Instead of heeding his plea, she cried even louder. *I do need to pick up a few things from the store.* Kent sighed. *I suppose it wouldn't hurt to stop off at the toy department and pick up a little something for her. She's had a hard day. We've both had a bad day.*

His thoughts shifted to Shauna again. *She's the reason for my daughter's bad day.*

Oh, but how Shauna's beautiful eyes had glistened as she had poured out her heart in the lobby of the day-care center. Her cheeks had flushed with a passionate glow as she laid out a plan for change. For some reason, her words and her passion left a lasting memory etched upon his seared conscience. *Was she right? Do I need to make some changes? Is Charity as bad as she seems to think?*

"Toy, Daddy!" Charity kicked the back of his seat, bringing him back to his senses. With his thoughts a jumbled mess, he turned the car in the direction of the store.

twelve

Shauna brushed away a loose tear as she struggled to bring some order to the classroom. "Children, pick up your toys. We're going to go to the playground."

As usual, most of the children chattered merrily as they picked up the colorful blocks and puzzle pieces. All but Charity, who refused to cooperate. Instead, she sulked in the corner.

Shauna gazed at the youngster, her heart twisting. *How could I not have noticed her bright green eyes—same as Kent's? And that round bulb of a nose? She's almost a duplicate, feature for feature.*

Charity yanked up a block into her tiny palm and threw it across the room, nearly hitting one of the other children. Shauna scolded her as she reached down to pick up the block. "Charity, be careful." When she did not receive a response, she added, "It's time to pick up."

"No." The youngster folded her arms. "No pick up. You."

Shauna shook her head, trying to imagine how someone as wonderful as Kent Chapman could possibly manage a handful like this.

Of course, he hadn't seemed so wonderful during their last exchange. In fact, he had been downright rude.

Well, maybe not rude—but irritated. And determined to prove her wrong. Was she wrong? Had she been too hard on his daughter? If she had known Charity was his little girl, would she have treated her differently? Would she have treated him differently?

Too late to worry about all of that now. Chances were pretty good Kent Chapman would never speak to her again. *If he doesn't, that's just childish. We can be friends, at the very least. Besides, someone has to be honest with him about his daughter. She's spoiled rotten. If I don't speak up, who will?* She glanced down at the youngster, who sat on the floor playing, completely ignoring Shauna's instruction.

"Charity, pick up your puzzle." This time, instead of raising her voice, Shauna walked over to the youngster and helped her with the task. Charity's cheeks blazed pink with excitement. "Outside! Play."

"Yes, we're going out right now. Just as soon as you finish picking up. That's what big girls do."

"Charity baby."

"Charity is a big girl. You're Daddy's big girl, and you're teacher's big girl, too." Shauna gave the warmest smile she could muster.

"I big girl. I pick up." Charity flew into action, scooping up puzzle pieces. She smiled as she finished. "Go outside now?"

"Yes, we go outside." Charity stood and reached for Shauna's hand.

Shauna led the little ones out to the playground, where they at once headed for the swings.

Soft-spoken Dinah gave Marisa her spot on the swings. Clay, ever the clown, made faces at the two of them, and they giggled, then told him to go away. He refused, choosing to tease them even more.

Precious Abigail climbed to the top of the slide but seemed hesitant to slide down until Joey and Jonathan came up behind her and insisted she give them a turn. McKinsey Chesterfield and petite Elizabeth Darby held hands and spun in a circle.

Bobby lingered behind, begging for a snack. When Shauna refused, he sauntered off to join Danny on the teeter-totter, though Bobby clearly weighed a good fifteen or twenty pounds more. Danny sat perched up in the air, all smiles—clearly happy to be the smaller of the two, since it put him in the higher position.

Sweet April Madison sat alone on the ground, playing with a doodlebug. And Charity, never one to rest on her laurels, made the rounds from child to child, demanding her turn on every piece of playground equipment. Shauna couldn't help but understand the children's frustration at the little girl.

I can't focus on her flaws. I have to stay positive.

Shauna turned her attention to Ellen, who entered the playground alone. "Are you on a break?"

"Nope." Ellen's brow wrinkled as she spoke. "Mrs. Fritz sent me out to keep an eye on your class for you."

"What do you mean?"

"She, uh, she wants to see you in her office." Ellen gestured toward the door, where Mrs. Fritz stood waiting.

"Did she say what she wanted?" Shauna whispered.

Ellen shook her head, and a sense of foreboding came over Shauna. She couldn't help but wonder at the seriousness in Mrs. Fritz's eyes. Rarely had she seen her with such a stern expression. *What in the world did I do?*

"Children, I'll be back in a few minutes," Shauna called out across the playground. "Mind Miss Ellen while I'm gone." With a deep breath, she turned and made her way toward the back door. She followed along behind Mrs. Fritz toward the front office like an obedient puppy. They walked inside the tiny room, and the older woman closed the door with a click.

"I know you're probably wondering why I've called you in here." The director settled herself into the chair behind the desk.

"Yes." Shauna could only manage the one word as she sat. Her nerves wouldn't allow much more. The clicking of the clock on the wall distracted her momentarily. Or was that the sound of her heart beating in her ears? She couldn't be quite sure. At any rate, she needed to stay focused.

"To be honest," Mrs. Fritz said, "I've been a little disappointed in your work these past few days. You haven't been yourself, and it shows."

"Really?" Shauna let her imagination run wild for a moment. "I've been working harder than ever, and there haven't been any unusual incidents with the children, so I'm not sure what you mean."

"What I mean," Mrs. Fritz gave her a thoughtful stare, "is that you haven't been happy. You've come across as a little sharp-tempered and uncaring, and that's out of character for you."

"I have?" Shauna's heart began to race. "I. . ."

"Some of the other teachers have noticed. And I've spent a little time observing you the past few days, as well."

"You have?"

"Perhaps. . .perhaps I made a mistake by placing you with the two-year-olds."

No mistaking her meaning there. "It is true that I've spent more time with the older ones, but I feel sure I can adapt what I learned in school. You said it yourself that first day— 'Children are children.'" Shauna felt tears well up.

"I'm concerned about your ability to connect with the little ones in your class." Mrs. Fritz's eyes narrowed a bit. "Just because you've studied children doesn't mean you have a natural way with them. That has to come with time and opportunity. I've wanted to give you that opportunity."

"Wanted to? Are you—are you firing me?" Tears spilled out onto her lashes now, and she brushed them away.

"Shauna. . ." Mrs. Fritz stood. "I don't want to be hurtful, but I feel I really must say something. You seem to struggle with your position here. You don't appear happy, and the children sense that."

"I'm happy with everything except. . ." Shauna's gaze shifted to the floor.

"Charity." Mrs. Fritz spoke the child's name softly, and tears tumbled down Shauna's cheeks.

"Yes. Charity. I can't get a handle on her. She doesn't like me, and I can't seem to get her to mind, no matter what I do. It's not that I haven't tried. I have. In fact, I lie in bed at night trying to think of ways to deal with her. I've tried everything. Absolutely everything. At least, everything I've been taught."

Mrs. Fritz leaned back in her chair and pursed her lips before finally speaking. "Has it occurred to you that she senses your dislike?"

"Dislike?" For a moment, Shauna thought about arguing but settled back into her chair, overcome with shame. *Lord, is that what it is? Do I really dislike her?*

A scripture came to mind at once, one she could not ignore: *"Whoever welcomes a little child like this in my name welcomes me. But if anyone causes one of these little ones who believe in me to sin, it would be better for him to have a large millstone hung around his neck and to be drowned in the depths of the sea."*

Regret washed over Shauna immediately. *Oh, Lord. Please forgive me, and help me to see her the way You do.*

Mrs. Fritz placed a gentle hand on Shauna's shoulder. "Some things just take time. And I want to give you the time to fall in love with Charity. It will happen, trust me. I've had dozens of tough cases through the years, and there were times I thought I'd quit before working with some of those children again."

"Really?" Shauna looked up in amazement. "You're so great

with all of the kids, even the hard ones. How did you do it?"

"It just takes time, honey. Pretty soon you'll fall so in love with them that leaving each day will be painful."

Was that possible? "I—I hope so." Shauna sighed.

"I know so," the older woman said with an encouraging nod. "And you'll have to trust me when I say that I didn't learn that in any university or classroom."

Ouch. Shauna looked down at her hands as she spoke. "Please give me another chance with Charity. I'll try harder. I will."

"I spoke to her father this morning. Mr. Chapman wants to make sure his daughter is not singled out—that she receives the same love and care as all the other children."

Shauna's stomach flip-flopped at the mention of Kent's name. Had he called to complain about her involvement? "If you give me time," she said, "things will get better. I'm sure of it. You won't be sorry."

"I hope not, honey." Mrs. Fritz gave her another concerned look. "That little girl has lost so much already. She needs all the love we can possibly pour out on her and more. We can't take the place of her mother, but we can show her what loving women are like so that she can grow up to be one."

Shauna's heart wrenched. "You're right." She pressed away the lump in her throat. "I know you're right. And from now on, I won't just tolerate Charity. I'll ask the Lord to give me a love for her."

Mrs. Fritz gave her a warm smile then patted her on the shoulder. "Now that's the kind of answer I was looking for. And don't be ashamed of the fact that you have to ask Him to give you that love. Sometimes it doesn't come naturally. One of these days, you'll have your own children, and your love for them will be overwhelming. Natural. But in cases like these, sometimes love has to grow. I predict Charity will learn to love you, too."

Shauna stood, and the older woman wrapped her in a warm embrace.

"It's pretty amazing what a little love will do," Mrs. Fritz said with a smile. "A little goes a long, long way."

Shauna drew in a deep breath and stepped toward the door, prepared to begin a new phase in her journey.

❧

Kent paced across the office, toying with the idea of calling Shauna. When his fractured nerves could take it no more, he picked up the telephone and punched in the number. Her phone rang four times before finally transitioning to the prerecorded message.

"I'm sorry I can't come to the phone right now," her cheery voice greeted him. "I'm probably hugging a child or teaching someone their ABCs. Leave a message, and I'll get back to you during nap time or after school."

With a lump in his throat, he left a raspy message. "Shauna. . .Shauna, this is Kent Chapman. I really need to talk to you. . ." His voice drifted off as he thought about what to say next. For some reason he couldn't seem to think clearly. Her beautiful smile seemed to penetrate his heart, making words impossible. "I. . .I. . . Could you call me back? This isn't really about Charity. I just wanted. . .needed to talk to you."

He clicked off, feeling like an idiot—not just for the choppy message but also the call he had made earlier this morning to Mrs. Fritz. Had he made a mistake by telephoning the school's director to offer critique? Had he come down too hard on Shauna? Maybe she just needed someone to help her understand Charity's special situation—her need for female role models.

Kent couldn't help but smile as he remembered Shauna on the night of their date. She had looked so happy to be with him—so carefree—and her eyes had twinkled merrily as they made their way into the restaurant.

Of course, there was that one part where she had commented on the unruly child. What was it she had said about parents allowing their children to get away with too much? And hadn't she complained about her job that night, letting him know that her situation at work was nearing the unbearable point? Could she have been talking about his daughter, or were there other things to be factored into the equation?

He sighed, knowing in his heart that he had, at least in part, spoiled Charity. In so many ways, he had made allowances for her behavior because of her situation.

Perhaps more than made allowances. In his heart, Kent had to acknowledge that he had played a role in the development of his daughter's poor habits.

I've given her everything she ever wanted. I've let her get away with far too much. I've allowed the temper tantrums to go on without really stopping to discipline. All because. . .

His thoughts shifted to Faith and tears stung his eyes. *I'll never know how Faith would have raised her. But I know what God is calling me to do. I have to raise her in the fear and admonition of the Lord. And if that means a little discipline. . .*

So be it.

thirteen

Kent stood outside his mother's bookstore, waiting for Shauna. His nerves were a jumbled mess. They had been, ever since her phone call agreeing to meet him. He fought to balance his feelings of guilt with his need to explain his daughter's behavior. *Lord, please give me the words to say. I don't want to blow this. I really like Shauna.*

I really like Shauna. For the first time, he found himself facing the truth of the matter. He liked Shauna. And he wanted Shauna to like—no, love—Charity. But he couldn't make that happen. Only the Lord could manage such a seemingly impossible task.

When Shauna's white Saturn pulled up, he walked to the driver's side and opened the door for her.

She seemed a bit surprised at his gesture but greeted him with a quiet, "Hello." Restrained. But he didn't blame her.

"Hello to you, too. Glad you could make it." Kent gave her a bright smile and led the way into the coffee shop at the back of the store. She followed behind in silence. He hoped to break it with the offer of something warm to drink. "Would you like some coffee?" He nodded toward the counter.

She gave a little shiver. "Yes. It's really getting chilly out there."

I sure hope it doesn't get chilly in here. "Almost feels like fall, doesn't it?"

Her lips curled up, the first hint at a smile. "I love our long summers, but I was happy to see that cold front come through. I was starting to think it would never happen."

"If you could call it a cold front." He chuckled. "In Houston, when it dips down into the sixties, we pull out our coats. I remember one winter it actually snowed about an inch. They let school out for the day." He chuckled, remembering.

"I was in second grade that year." Her face lit up. "We tried to build a snowman, but it melted before we could get it put together."

"We tried the snowman thing, too," Kent said. "Isn't it weird to think we were probably building snowmen at the same time just a few miles apart from each other?" They stared at each other for a moment in silence.

"Building puddles was more like it," Shauna said, finally. "By midafternoon the temperature had risen into the fifties, and our front yard was a muddy mess."

"I remember that." He gave her a curious look. "That's Houston for you. Just about the time you think you stand a chance at a real winter, a heat wave appears." He grinned.

She pulled her sweater a little tighter and nodded toward the counter. "Speaking of which. . .let's get that coffee."

"Sure. And maybe when we're done, I can show you around the bookstore. My mom manages the place."

"She does?" Shauna's face lit up, and he couldn't but notice the sparkle in her eyes. "That's right! I remember hearing that Charity's grandmother ran a bookstore. I love them. Always have. Especially the kids' section."

"They've got a great one here. I'll show you everything after we visit for a while."

They walked to the counter and, much to his surprise, Shauna ordered a Pumpkin Latte—something he would never have considered. He chose the usual Mocha Java. With beverages in hand, they made their way through the crowd to a tiny table in the back of the room. Nearly each table along the way was abuzz with activity. People sat holding laptops, typing madly. Others talked on cell phones. Some sat alone, reading the newspaper or a book.

Kent and Shauna finally located a small table in the back of the room, and they sat down face-to-face. No longer could they avoid speaking to one another. *This wall has to come down.*

Shauna took a sip of her drink then fanned her mouth. "*Ew,* that's hot."

"Careful." Kent smiled, thinking of how many times he had used that same word with Charity. *Careful, honey! Don't spill. Careful, baby. Watch what you're doing!*

"I always manage to do that." Shauna set the drink down on the table to let it cool off.

Silence enveloped them again, and Kent knew he must dive in or they might never speak again. He began the conversation with a random thought. "This is a strange time to be living," he said as he glanced around the room.

"What do you mean?"

Kent gestured around the room, slightly distracted by all of the conversations going on around him. "Look around you," he said. "Half the folks in this room are talking to people they're not even with and ignoring the ones they are with."

She looked first right, then left, then slowly nodded. "You're right. I guess I never thought about it that way before."

"I think about it all the time. We don't have a lot of time with the people we love these days. And when we are together, sometimes we don't really connect."

She sighed. "I know what you mean. By the time I get home from work, I don't really spend a lot of time talking to my parents. They're busy. I'm busy. Or I'm on the Internet checking my e-mail." Her cheeks flushed slightly as she mentioned the last part.

Talking to her boyfriend, perhaps? Why did that idea suddenly hurt so much? Kent struggled to understand his own feelings, mixed-up as they were.

"I hear you," he said finally. "It's just a shame, you know? We've got people right in front of us, and we don't always take the time to tell them how much they mean to us—or even to relate to them at all." He paused. "I guess I'm just sensitive to this because there are so many things I wish I'd said to Faith before she died. You know, I never told her how pretty she looked on that day. She had fixed her hair a different way, and I never even commented on it."

"I'm sure she knew. . ." Shauna gave him a sympathetic look. "She knew you loved her, and women who know they're loved don't always need to hear those things."

"Still, it's important to take the opportunity when we have it."

He could see a look of pain in Shauna's eyes, and he wondered if she had misinterpreted his words. She began to speak, and he felt sure she had.

"Speaking of opportunities," Shauna glanced down at the table, "I just wanted to start by saying how sorry I am for coming down so hard on Charity." She looked up, and he noticed the glistening of tears in her eyes. "I'm ashamed and a little embarrassed to admit that I'm on such a learning curve. There are so many things I still can't handle. . ."

"I understand," Kent said. "Maybe more than I let on. I know how hard she can be, trust me. She wears me out sometimes."

"Really? You're not just saying that?" Shauna gave him a weary look.

"It's hard enough to be a parent," he explained. "Even harder to be a single parent who works all day at a brand new job. I haven't had a good night's sleep for a really long time. It's not because I'm not tired, that's for sure. I'm exhausted."

"I hear you. By the time I get home from work, I just want to fall into bed and forget about the day. I've learned a lot over the past few weeks. It's one thing to talk about working with children. It's another thing to actually work with them."

Kent's heart felt heavy, and he knew there were still words he must speak, as well. "You've apologized to me, but I need to do the same."

"Why?" An expression of curiosity crossed her face. "What did you do?"

"I overreacted that day at the school, and I—I telephoned Mrs. Fritz."

"Ah." She nodded. "I knew that. She told me. But she didn't come down too hard on me. In fact, we had a really pleasant conversation. She helped me put things in perspective."

"Sometimes I wish I had someone to help me do that," Kent said. "Besides just my mom, I mean. She's great, but I really miss having someone like. . ." His words drifted away, and he looked down at the table then took a sip of his coffee.

"Your wife?" Shauna looked him in the eye.

Kent nodded. "I need help. I can't do this alone. And I'm so worried that Charity will grow up without the influence of a mother. Maybe she'll be a tomboy. Or maybe kids will make fun of her because I'm so clueless about her wardrobe. And what am I going to do when she grows up? I can't talk to her about all of that—that. . .girl stuff."

He shook his head, and Shauna chuckled. "You're getting a little ahead of yourself, Dad." She smiled, and his heart flip-flopped as she continued on. "You should probably just take one day at a time."

"Very biblical advice," he agreed. "And I do my best. But

there are times I feel like a complete failure." He hung his head in shame. "Like the other day when you pointed out all of your struggles with Charity. I felt so. . ."

"Helpless?" She drew in a deep breath as he nodded.

"Yes."

"I feel terrible for making you feel that way." She gave him a look of genuine caring. "I just didn't know what else to do. And I've asked myself over and over again if I would have handled the situation differently if I had known you were her father. After all. . ." She paused, and he thought he saw a hint of a smile in her eyes.

"What?"

"Well. . ." She stammered a bit then looked up at him with a hopeful expression. "We were getting to know each other, and I. . .I really liked that."

"Me, too." He couldn't help but smile.

Shauna's eyes lit up, and she spoke with renewed determination. "I'm going to try a lot harder with Charity. I promise you that—and not just because she's your daughter, but because it's the right thing to do."

"And I need to make you a promise, too," Kent added. "I'll work on being more disciplined with her," he added. "And not spoiling her so much."

"Sounds like a plan." Shauna nodded her agreement, and they sat in silence a moment before he asked the question that had weighed on his heart for a while now. "So where does that leave us?"

She shrugged and gave a bashful smile. "Is it okay just to start over?"

"I'd like that." Kent suddenly felt as if a weight had been lifted.

"Me, too." Shauna's cheeks flushed as she took a sip of her

coffee and Kent settled back in his chair, heart swelling with pure joy.

❧

Shauna's coffee grew cool as she sat across from Kent Chapman. She listened with great interest as he talked about his unique relationship with Charity. For the first time, she saw the child through his eyes—the good traits and bad, humorous and serious. She heard the details of her upbringing, the role her grandparents played, and the great lack of not having a mother. She heard about Charity's love for music and her desire to dance. She laughed as Kent shared his fears about his daughter dating one day. This somehow shifted into a discussion she had not anticipated.

"I don't think I like the idea of dating very much."

She shrugged. "Never did much of it myself." She started to explain that Joey was her first serious boyfriend but decided against it.

"What is your ideal man like?" Kent looked her squarely in the eye as he asked the question.

Shauna gulped down a mouthful of coffee and fought to answer. She wanted to say, "Someone like Joey," but right now that answer didn't sound right, even to her own ears.

"My ideal man"—she stumbled a bit—"will obviously be someone who loves children."

"Obviously." He smiled.

"And he's got to be someone who's strong in the Lord. Someone who can lead our family. That's a critical part of the equation."

"So you're interested in having children, then." Kent's eyes seemed to smile as she nodded.

"Of course."

"Ah." He nodded. "Go ahead."

She went on to explain that her husband would be the kind of man who would encourage her to fulfill her dreams. Then she turned the question around on him. "Now tell me what the perfect woman looks like to you."

An immediate look of pain filled his eyes, and she realized he must be thinking of Faith. "Other than my wife," he said slowly, "I'd have to say that the perfect woman has to be someone who shares my love for church-related things. I've always worked with teens, and she would have to support me in that."

"I was president of my youth group when I was sixteen." *What are you doing? Promoting yourself?* Her cheeks warmed immediately, and she hoped he didn't get the wrong idea. *Is it a wrong idea?*

"I was way too into myself when I was sixteen," Kent shook his head, and she could read the sadness in his eyes. "I wasted a lot of time in that regard—but to answer your question, I was always looking for the perfect woman, even before I knew the Lord."

"So does that mean you dated a lot when you were younger?" Shauna asked.

Kent groaned. "Yeah."

"Explain."

She sensed a story coming but couldn't help laughing as he shared the details of his youth. "I guess you could say I was always a flirt."

"Really?"

"Yes. I always fell in love too easily. If you don't believe me, just ask my mom or my sister. Most of the time the girls didn't even know I existed."

"That's hard to picture."

Kent's cheeks flushed. "Well, I made a fool of myself more than once. We'll just leave it at that. I guess that's why I was so surprised when Faith took an interest in me. You have to trust me when I say that I don't see myself as the kind of guy women would find. . .appealing. I'm pretty. . .ordinary."

"But ordinary is appealing," Shauna argued. "N–not that you're ordinary. I'm not saying that. Most women, me included, aren't looking for super-heroes—just a man who will love them for who they are."

The room grew eerily silent as Kent flashed a crooked smile. Shauna's heart lurched. She couldn't seem to wipe the grin from her own face, but the guilt that quickly followed wiped it away. *Lord, please take these feelings away. I need to stay focused on You and Your plan for my life. If Joey is the man You have for me, settle the issue in my heart once and forever while he's here. If not. . .*

A picture of Charity flashed before her eyes, and she struggled with the emotions that followed. *Lead me in Your way, Lord. I don't want to follow my feelings or emotions. I just want what You want for me, no more and no less.*

Her thoughts shifted to the day care, and she felt a peace. Except for Charity, the children seemed to have taken to her. Shauna's heart warmed as she thought about how much a part of her heart they had become, as well. Grafted in. The words came to her slowly, and she repeated them to herself. *Grafted in.* Sort of like God had grafted in His children.

Could she do the same with a little monster like Charity Chapman? Only time would tell. In the meantime, she would be content to tour the bookstore with one of the nicest men she'd met in a long, long time.

fourteen

Kent pushed the cart through the grocery store, trying to ignore Charity's whining. "Buy cookies, Daddy!"

"Not this time, honey," he said. "I need to buy milk and cereal."

His cell phone rang, and he tried to balance it against his ear with his shoulder as he continued to push the cart. "Hello?"

"Pastor Chapman?"

The muscles in his jaw tightened immediately. *Vicky Ebert. How did she get my cell number?* "Yes?"

"This is Vicky. I hate to interrupt whatever you're doing, but I really need to talk to you. It's important."

"How did you. . .?"

"I hope you don't mind that I called you on your cell phone," she interjected. "I called the church secretary at home and told her it was an emergency."

Great. "What's happened?" Kent asked. "Is something wrong with one of the boys?" Kent continued to push the cart through the health-and-beauty department and on towards the dairy section. Charity chattered on and on, but he tried to force his thoughts to the matter at hand.

"No, it's not that," Vicky said. "The boys are fine. Well, as fine as boys without a father can be. I'm the one with the problem, actually." She paused definitively. "Josh has checked himself into a program."

Kent stopped his cart in the middle of the aisle so that he could take the time to respond appropriately. "Vicky, that's wonderful. I'm so glad to hear it."

She sighed. "But don't you see, Pastor? This just complicates things."

"It does?" Kent tried to make sense of her words. In the meantime, Charity reached to pull a large bag of women's personal products down off the shelf and into their basket. Kent shook his head and mouthed the word *no* as he lifted the item back to the shelf. "How does this complicate things, Vicky? I don't get it."

"He's in a Christian program," she explained, "and they want to see him restored. At least, that's what they call it. Restored."

"Of course. Isn't that what you want?"

"Well, I do want him to stop drinking," she said. "But that doesn't necessarily mean I want him to come back home again, even if he does get a handle on the alcohol. He's awful with the boys and with me."

"When he drinks, you mean." Kent pushed the cart a few feet forward to keep Charity from reaching out for more embarrassing items. "But you know what, Vicky? He wasn't always like that. I remember Josh as a teen—just a few years ago. He was really on fire for the Lord. It wasn't until after his father's suicide that he began to crater."

"Still," she argued. "There's no guarantee he will change. Drunk or sober."

Kent rounded the corner, horrified to see he had landed on the sweets aisle.

"Candy, Daddy!" Charity shouted. "We buy candy!"

To keep her quiet, he tossed a bag of her favorite candy into the basket. She reached for it immediately, but he pressed it to the back of the basket.

Charity began to cry. "Candy, candy!"

Kent raised his voice so that Vicky could hear him above his daughter's outburst. "There are no guarantees," he said. "But don't you think it's worth taking a chance? Especially if Josh has checked himself into a program. That means he's taking this more seriously."

"I guess." She didn't sound terribly convinced.

Kent spoke with great passion, borne out of understanding. "God can intervene in Josh's situation, Vicky. I know He can, because I know He delivered me from a drinking problem years ago."

"He—He did?"

"Yes." Kent pushed the cart beyond the candy section, still headed towards dairy. "You didn't know me very well when I was a teenager. We hung out in completely different crowds. But I was pretty messed up. Then God got ahold of me and everything changed. The person I used to be no longer existed. And all of the things I did before are in the past."

"That's great," she said. "I just never knew."

Kent's ear grew warm, so he shifted the phone to the other ear as he wrapped up his thoughts. "There's a scripture I love. It goes something like this, 'But one thing I do: Forgetting what is behind and straining toward what is ahead.' " He finished with great zeal. " 'I press on toward the goal to win the prize for which God has called me heavenward in Christ Jesus.' "

Vicky began to sniffle. "I just want a man who will love me and love my kids."

Kent stopped the basket, opened the bag of candies, and handed one to Charity, whose face lit up like a Christmas tree. "I understand that," he said, convinced the Lord was speaking through him. "You're only asking for the very thing Josh promised you on your wedding day. But Vicky, I'm really going to encourage you to give this relationship with your husband another chance. If he's making an effort to become a new man, maybe God will give you what you've been asking for all along."

"Do you really think that's possible?" Kent heard her blow her nose. "Really?"

"I do, because I've walked a mile in Josh's shoes. And I'm awfully glad my family didn't give up on me. There's no telling where I'd be today if they had." Kent ran his fingers through Charity's hair, and she cradled her head into his hand. "I wouldn't give this advice in every case," he was quick to add. "But I really feel the Lord is laying these words on my heart. Love can overcome even the biggest of obstacles."

Charity reached out her arms, wanting to be held. He scooped her up out of the basket, and she threw her arms around his neck in a tight embrace.

"I guess you're right." Vicky's tears seemed to have dried up now. "I guess I'm just so scared to believe that something so. . . impossible sounding. . .can actually happen."

"That's where faith comes in," Kent said. *Faith.* He pressed Charity a little tighter to himself. "Believing the impossible."

Vicky sighed. "I know you're right."

Her end of the phone grew silent, and Kent knew the conversation had drawn to its rightful conclusion. "I have to let you go, Vicky. I'm in the store with Charity, and we need some father-daughter time. Go and love on those boys of yours. They need you right now."

"Okay." Her voice brightened. "I'll do that. And. . .thanks, Pastor."

"No problem," he said. "But next time, Vicky, it might be better if you called on one of the women in the church. They're probably a little more qualified than I am to discuss the things you're thinking and feeling. They could give you a woman's perspective, at any rate."

"I'll do that. Thanks again." As the line went dead, Kent tucked his phone into his pocket. Charity laid her head on his shoulder, and he ran his fingers through her hair.

"How's Daddy's girl?" He asked. "You doing okay?"

"I okay." She looked up with an impish grin. "I like candy."

"I know you do." He lifted her up to place her back into the basket. Only at this point did he notice the chocolate smeared all over his shirt.

For once, it simply didn't matter.

❧

When the doorbell rang on the second Saturday in November, Shauna happened to be the only one at home. Her parents, ever the world travelers, had taken their RV to the nearby town of New Braunfels for the weekend.

Nothing could have prepared her for the shock of discovering who stood on the other side of the door.

"J–Joey?"

His lopsided grin widened into a full-fledged smile. "Hey, you!" He embraced her warmly and planted a tender kiss on her cheek, one that would have warmed her heart and brought a smile to her own face just a few short weeks ago. "Long time, no see."

Now, however, she could not be sure what feelings gripped her heart. Fear? Confusion? An odd sense of betrayal?

"Come in, come in." She grabbed him by the hand and ushered him into the living room, eyes never leaving his. "What are you doing here?"

"Don't you think it's about time I came for a visit?" He slipped an arm around her waist.

If you had asked me that a few weeks ago, I would have said yes, but now. . .

Now she couldn't seem to collect her thoughts or make sense of the conversation. "How long are you here?"

"I have to be back in school after the Thanksgiving holidays."

"Thanksgiving? You're staying all week?"

"If you'll have me." He planted a kiss on her lips, and the old feelings returned immediately. She could hardly think clearly or make sense of his sudden appearance. "Now. . ." his voice lowered considerably, "where are these parents of yours? I have to make a good first impression."

"They're out of town until Tuesday. My mom wanted to be back in time for Thanksgiving, so if you're staying that long. . ."

"We've got the place to ourselves, then." He grinned mischievously. "I couldn't have planned things any better."

"Joey." Shauna gave him a look she hoped he would not ignore. "You know better than that. Don't you have someplace else you can stay?"

He shrugged and grew silent for a moment. "I guess I could stay with my brother and his wife. But those kids of theirs are terrors."

"Hey now, watch how you talk about children." She grinned. "I happen to love them, you know."

"If you love them"—he drew her close—"then I'll learn to love them, too."

He kissed her a bit more passionately this time, and she pulled away, a little stunned.

"Joey, I haven't seen you for weeks. And you've hardly even answered my e-mails."

"I know." He sighed. "I'm in over my head with my school. It's not like it was with my undergraduate classes. I'm really having to work now."

"But still. . ."

"I should have written more often." He stepped back a

bit to gaze wistfully into her eyes. Her heart fluttered as he continued on. "I let myself get too caught up in my work, and I almost forgot the most important thing."

Shauna smiled, in spite of herself. "The most important thing?" She leaned her head into his chest.

"All of my hard work will seem kind of pointless if I don't have someone to share it with." He drew her close once again. "I've had time to think a lot more clearly—and time to pray. I like what the Lord is showing me. A lot." His eyes shimmered with an excitement that seemed intriguing, yet unusual.

"Really?"

He nodded. "Yes. And I've missed you a lot more than I've let on. I should have told you before now."

Yes, you should have. Instead of scolding, she gazed up into his eyes. Kind eyes. Loving eyes.

Eyes she could grow to appreciate once again.

fifteen

Kent stood before the people of Grace Community Church preparing to deliver a life changing sermon. However, he struggled to stay focused on the message the Lord had laid on his heart. Looking out onto the faces of several hundred parishioners, his eyes seemed only to land on one.

Better make that two. Shauna Alexander sat so close to the shockingly handsome blond guy on her left that Kent had to conclude the most likely possibility: *That must be Joey.*

He forced his thoughts to the matter at hand. *Stay focused, man. Don't get distracted from what God has for these folks. Lord, forgive me. I want to keep my heart pure and my focus on You. I know that You have a message to deliver to Your people this morning.*

In fact, he had been up half the night, listening to the voice of the Holy Spirit, rewriting an earlier message crafted days prior. The words *inner healing* had taken on a whole new meaning as the Lord had laid out a blueprint involving appropriate scriptures, biblical examples, and personal experience stories. It had all seemed so clear in the night. But this morning, with far too little sleep and far too many distractions, he struggled to stay focused.

Lord, I know You have a plan for this morning. Don't let me get in the way, Father. Keep my eyes on You.

With a renewed sense of direction, Kent opened his Bible and began to speak. He poured out his heart with each word. As he shared, he couldn't help but realize the Lord had crafted this message just for him. *Is that why You kept me up through the night, Lord? Are You reminding me of all the work You've already done in my life?*

Kent quoted the scripture of choice from Psalm 34: "The Lord is close to the brokenhearted and saves those who are crushed in spirit. A righteous man may have many troubles, but the Lord delivers him from them all." As he spoke the words, he reflected on his own heart, and how the Lord had healed him from the pain of Faith's death, how the Lord had lifted Kent's eyes and placed them back where they belonged—on his relationship with God.

Kent looked out over his congregation, aware that many dabbed their eyes. One woman's face seemed awash with tears. A few others sniffled. As he drew his remarks to a close, he offered an invitation to those who struggled with heartbreak to give their hearts—and their situations—to the Lord. Many came forward for prayer. Still others knelt at their seats or sat quietly with heads bowed.

By the time the final worship song had been sung, Kent heard the Lord's voice of approval over the morning: *"Well done, My child."*

As he made his way through the people, Kent couldn't help but marvel at their remarks. Many spoke to him with tears fresh in their eyes. "Pastor Kent, you spoke straight to my heart and made me face some things I haven't seen willing to face for years. Gave me hope that things can get better."

On and on the comments flowed. Kent found himself overwhelmed with the way God had apparently used him—an ordinary, flawed, unschooled man—to minister to His people. *What are you trying to teach me here, Lord?* He felt his heart stirred as never before and could not deny the Lord appeared to be doing something brand-new in his life.

Kent traveled through the crowd until at least he saw his mother and stepfather at the back of the auditorium. His mother wrapped him in her arms as she whispered words of encouragement into his ear. "I'm so proud of you." Her eyes brimmed over. "You were listening."

He gave her a quizzical look. "Listening?"

She pointed up and he nodded, understanding. "Ah. Yes. It feels really good."

"And God truly spoke through you," she continued. "That makes my heart smile."

"Everything makes your heart smile, Mom."

A light tap on his shoulder caused him to turn away from his mother for a moment. Kent caught his breath as he came face-to-face with Shauna. "Hey."

"Hey." She gave him a winsome smile. "I didn't mean to interrupt your conversation."

"No problem. I wanted to introduce you to my mother, anyway."

His mom extended her hand and smiled broadly. "So this is the wonderful teacher I've heard so much about."

Shauna groaned audibly, and Kent responded with an inward grimace, hoping his mother would choose not to repeat some of Charity's more pointed descriptions of her teacher.

Fortunately, his mother continued on with some encouraging words. "We have our hands full with just one toddler. I don't know how in the world you manage an entire classroom full of them."

"I'm afraid I don't do the best job of it sometimes." Shauna's gaze shifted downward, and Kent fought to think of something to say to redirect the conversation.

"Charity's learned so much from you." He smiled. "She came home reciting the alphabet the other day."

"She's very bright." Shauna's face lit up.

The young man next to her cleared his throat, and Shauna's cheeks blazed with apparent embarrassment. "Oh, I'm so sorry. I forgot to introduce you. Kent, this is Joey Klein. Joey, Pastor Kent Chapman."

Kent responded to the fellow's enthusiastic handshake but had to wonder about Shauna's formality. *Pastor Kent Chapman?* Somehow the phrase felt oddly uncomfortable coming from her. Far too formal for two people so closely acquainted. He quickly introduced Joey to his mother and Andrew.

"Nice to meet you all." Joey slipped his arm around Shauna's waist. "I've heard about how friendly this church is. Now I've seen it for myself."

You have? "We're happy to have you." Kent spoke with sincerity.

"And I'm glad to finally have the chance to come for a visit." Joey pulled Shauna a little closer. "It's been way too long. I've missed this girl of mine."

Shauna looked a little nervous as she added to his sentence. "Joey's here for the holidays. He came to meet my parents."

Meeting her parents. Sounds serious. "Well, I hope you enjoy your trip." With an unusually heavy heart, Kent looked into Shauna's eyes. *So this is the guy. This is the one you write e-mails to.*

"I've cooked a roast," his mother interjected with great enthusiasm. "Enough for an army. Why don't you all come over for lunch?" She reached to squeeze Shauna's hand. "I'd be so happy to have you. And I know Charity would love it."

"That's really nice of you," Joey spoke with determination, "but we've already got plans. I'm taking Shauna out for a steak dinner." His lips curled up in a smile.

They all nodded politely and parted ways with positive comments, but as he stepped away from Shauna, Kent's heart twisted a bit. *Calm down, man. You've certainly got no claim on her. And if Joey is the man God has in mind for her. . .*

For some reason, his thoughts stopped right there.

❧

Shauna felt strangely uncomfortable as she climbed into Joey's car. Something about the look in Kent Chapman's eyes—a soulful look—had stirred her heart. Had she offended him in some way? She worked her way back through the conversation but could think of nothing that should have stirred up frustration or pain.

If he's still upset at me about Charity, then that's just silly. I thought we had all that settled the other night.

The other night. For some reason her heart wrenched as she remembered their conversation at the coffee shop. How wonderful that night had been. How comfortable. And how uncomfortable she felt right now. *Lord, what are You doing here?*

As Joey put the car into gear and headed out onto the interstate, she allowed her thoughts to wander even more. The night she and Kent had laughed over cups of coffee had more than broken the ice between them. Truly, they had forgiven one another for the way they had handled themselves that day at the school. She smiled, remembering his stories about Charity.

"Everything okay?"

She startled at Joey's voice. "Oh, yeah. . . I'm just a little preoccupied."

"Thinking about that sermon?"

"What do you mean?" She gazed at Joey with some degree of curiosity.

"I thought maybe he hit a trigger point."

She pursed her lips and shook her head. "Nope. No deep

inner turmoil in need of healing in this heart." She smiled in his direction but immediately wondered at the feelings of confusion that caused her chest to tighten. *Lord, am I in turmoil?*

"That's good." He reached for her hand, giving it a squeeze. "Because I don't want anything to distract you today."

"Today? What do you mean?"

"You'll see." He winked and flashed a whimsical smile.

They arrived at the restaurant less than ten minutes later. After parking, Joey rounded the car to open the door for Shauna. As always, she found herself relaxing as she looked into his eyes. *He really is a gentleman.* As they entered the restaurant, he once again opened the door.

"Thank you, kind sir."

He bowed rather dramatically. "You're welcome, my queen."

She blushed at his compliment.

The hostess seated them at the table, and Joey ordered for them both—with an unusual flair, she noted. Just as the salads arrived, he grew quite nervous.

"Are you sick?" she whispered.

He shook his head, not uttering a word.

"Are you sure?" Shauna reached for her fork but never shifted her gaze from his wrinkled brow.

He nodded slowly, almost methodically, then slipped out of his chair.

He looks as white as a ghost. "The bathroom is that way." She pointed to her right.

Joey never even looked up. Instead, he dropped to one knee and took her hand, his hand now trembling in her own.

"What in the world? Joey?"

"Shauna, I have something to ask you."

She couldn't help but notice his palm sweating. She also

noticed the amused looks on the faces of those seated nearby as they watched intently. "What are you doing?" she whispered.

"I'm trying to ask you something." He reached into his pocket and pulled out a tiny box.

As he opened it, her heart sailed into her throat. "Joey."

"Shauna," he looked up into her eyes, "I know I don't deserve you, but you would make me so happy"—his eyes filled with tears—"if you would marry me."

"I—I. . ." *Lord, is this the answer to my prayers from weeks ago? Is this really Your answer?*

She looked into Joey's eyes, filled with amazement. And filled with something else, as well.

A firm sense of knowing. . .

. . .that this was that last question on earth she could answer with a yes.

sixteen

Shauna brushed aside a few stray tears as she dressed for work. In the week since Joey's leaving, she had cried herself to sleep nearly every night. A thousand times she had questioned her decision to turn down Joey's request. A thousand times she had prayed, asking the Lord to guide her and to bring a sense of peace. But her peace, however real in some fleeting moments, seemed to be all mixed up with the guilt of hurting Joey.

"How did this happen? How did I end up hurting him? Lord, I never wanted to do that. And yet, how could I marry someone I'm clearly not in love with?"

She pondered those words. In her heart, she had to face the truth. She was not in love with Joey. Perhaps she never had been. *Maybe I was in love with the idea of being in love—not with an actual person. So what does love really feel like? And how will I know it when it comes?*

A picture of Kent's smiling face cheered her heart right away. If only love were as easy—as comfortable—as being with Kent. Sitting with a cup of coffee in her hand, talking about life. Talking about family. Talking about little girls dancing around the living room in imaginary tutus. If only. . .

The "if onlys" wrapped around her heart and squeezed tightly until she knew beyond a shadow of a doubt why being with Kent felt so comfortable. In spite of her problems with Charity, in spite of her confusion over Joey—in spite of everything, she had developed feelings for Kent Chapman.

But how could she trust her feelings? Hadn't they betrayed her before? *Lord, please forgive me. What I'm feeling is wrong. Kent has never expressed any romantic interest in me. And Charity. . .she still hasn't warmed up to me. Maybe she never will.*

Her mother tapped on the bedroom door then stuck her head inside. "Are you okay, honey?" Her eyes reflected great caring.

"I will be." Shauna sighed.

"Your father and I are worried about you." Her mother stepped into the room. "Is there anything we can do?"

Shauna shook her head. "I'll be fine after awhile. I guess I just need time to absorb everything." She sat on the edge of the bed and looked up into her mother's eyes. "Mom?"

"What?" Her mother sat next to her.

She gave her mom an imploring look. "Have you ever prayed for something—something you thought you really wanted—only to get it and then decide you didn't want it?"

Her mom chuckled. "Sort of, although I guess my little story probably won't measure up to what you're dealing with." She paused and smiled. "When I was a kid, I begged my mom for a puppy. I prayed for months. Finally, I got the very thing I prayed for—a tiny little thing with black and white fur."

Shauna looked at her curiously. "I don't think I've ever heard this story before."

"It's not one I'm very proud of," her mother continued. "I did pretty well with him at first. But he was unruly. Didn't want to be housetrained. Ruined my mother's furniture. Dug holes in the yard. Grew so large he outweighed me." She shrugged. "In the end, my mother ended up taking care of him for me. She fed him, bathed him, everything. She fell in love with that dog, thank goodness, but I never did. Funny thing was, I really, really wanted him."

"Or at least you thought you did." Shauna shrugged. "I know what that feels like. I thought I wanted someone like Joey. . . ."

"Maybe the words 'someone like Joey' are key here," her mother interjected. "Maybe the problem wasn't the idea—maybe it was the person."

Shauna shrugged then stood to slip on her jacket. "It's ironic you should say that. I was just thinking the same thing. But it's all so confusing. How do you know when the right person comes along if you can't trust what you're feeling?"

"Feelings will betray you," her mother said. "But God won't."

Shauna sighed. "I just feel like I've wasted so much time. It's crazy to think I spent so much time thinking I had Mr. Right, only to figure out he was Mr. Wrong for me."

Her mother patted her on the arm. "Happens all the time, honey. But don't think of it as wasted time. Any time you've learned a lesson or two, your time hasn't been wasted. And I guarantee you, Joey has learned a few lessons from this, as well. His heart might hurt a little now, but imagine how much more it would hurt years from now if he had actually married someone the Lord never intended for him to marry."

"I never thought of it that way." Shauna stood and ran a brush through her hair. "But let's not talk about marriage, okay? I think I've spent way too much time thinking about that lately and not enough time focusing on my work."

"True." Her mother stood alongside her. "But don't rule out the possibility of God's intervention in your love life, honey. Sometimes He walks us strategically down one road just to lead us to another."

Shauna turned to argue the point, but the twinkle in her mother's eye diverted her. *What is she up to?*

"Have a good day at work, honey. And don't hurry home on our account. Daddy and I have a Sunday school party tonight."

Is she trying to tell me something?

As Shauna climbed into the car to head off to work, the telephone rang. She recognized Ellen's voice on the other end.

"Shauna?"

"Hey, what's up?"

"Just thought you'd like to know we've, uh"—Ellen cleared her throat—"run into a small hitch up here."

Shauna groaned. Though Mrs. Fritz looked after the early morning crowd, Shauna had certainly heard of their antics on more than one occasion. "What's happened?"

"Bobby Radisson brought an apple from home, and Clay took it from him," Ellen explained.

"That's not much of a story." Shauna smiled and added a teasing comment. "Can't you come up with something better than that?"

"Yep. Clay flushed the apple down the toilet."

Shauna groaned. "Oh no."

"Oh no, is right," Ellen continued. "The toilet backed up, and the entire back section of the building is under about three inches of water."

Shauna's second "oh no" was a little more exaggerated than the first. "What are we going to do?"

"Mrs. Fritz has moved the infants into one room and toddlers into another. You'll be working with the three- and four-year-old teachers today in the lunchroom. Just wanted to let you know in advance so you wouldn't be startled when you got here."

Shauna groaned. "I was hoping for a quiet day."

"Around here?" Ellen laughed. "You should know better than that."

"I know, I know. But I really need it."

"Sounds like you need more than that," Ellen said. "Would

you like to go to dinner with me tonight? Sounds like you could use a friend."

"I'd like that." Shauna couldn't help but wonder at the Lord's timing. "And you're right. I do need a friend right now."

"Well, I'm here for you." Ellen paused. "At least I will be, just as soon as I get this casserole into the oven."

"We can talk when I get there," Shauna said. "And thanks for the warning. I'm just grateful Charity wasn't involved this time."

"She's getting better, you know. The terrible twos don't last forever."

As Ellen hung up, Shauna pondered her final words. Charity's antics, however bad, weren't completely out of character for a two-year-old. And the others certainly had the capability of acting up, as well. This morning's incident should more than settle that issue in her mind.

And Charity would outgrow this stage. Surely. Shauna found herself praying for the child, asking the Lord to help the little girl overcome the obstacles in her life.

Then, Shauna's prayers shifted. She began to pray for Kent Chapman—slowly at first, then with a passion borne from a heart now free to express itself. As the words flowed, the Lord filled her with a sense of overwhelming peace.

Shauna prayed for Kent's broken heart. She prayed for his relationship with Charity. She prayed for his job at the church and the many challenges he faced daily. She thanked the Lord for saving him from the choices he made as a teen.

And she prayed he would find himself as open to a new relationship. . .as she now found herself.

❧

Kent picked up the telephone and entered Shauna's number. What he would say when she answered, he had no idea. One thing was clear, he had to stop her from making a mistake with Joey—had to keep her from spending even one more day with the wrong man.

Just before the phone began to ring, he snapped his phone shut. "It's not my place. I have no right telling her something like that. She'll think I'm crazy. It's not like we're. . ." *a couple.*

His heart ached as the truth emerged. He didn't want Shauna to make the mistake of a lifetime, but what could he do? *Should I tell her how I feel? How do I feel?*

He took a few moments to analyze his heart. After all he had been through, why would the Lord send such new, exciting feelings to sweep over him? In fact, they were so new, so fresh, that they frightened him. And yet, he could not deny the truth—he didn't want Shauna to connect herself with any man, except himself. If she settled on anything less, it might very well break his heart.

"Lord, if this is really of You, then I ask for the impossible. I ask for You to protect her from the wrong relationship and lead her into the right one. And show me what to do, Father. . .and what not to do."

seventeen

"Charity?" Shauna looked at the youngster curiously.

Unusually quiet, the little girl sat in the corner, staring at a puzzle but not touching it. Instead, she rubbed at her arms, brow wrinkled, and lips curled into a pout.

"Charity, are you okay?" Shauna knelt down next to her, wondering at the red-rimmed watery eyes.

"I want my daddy."

"Oh, honey. . ." Shauna ran her hand through Charity's curls, "Are you missing your daddy?"

Charity nodded then rubbed at her arms again. "Go home." A lone tear trickled down the youngster's cheek.

"It's not even lunchtime," Shauna explained. "But I'm sure we'll have a fun day together. Why don't you play with your puzzle like the other boys and girls?" She began to fit a couple of the pieces together, but Charity shoved them aside and began to cry with full-fledged tears.

"I want my daddy." The little one now clawed at her arms, and curiosity got the better of Shauna.

"Can I see your arms?" She rolled up Charity's sleeves and gasped as her gaze fell on several tiny sores. "What in the world. . . ?"

"Arms hurt." Charity scratched at the spots.

Shauna quickly pulled down Charity's sleeves then placed a palm on the child's forehead, suspicions mounting. *She's burning up.* Shauna reached for the walkie-talkie and signaled the front office with great concern.

"Mrs. Fritz?"

The director's voice crackled a bit over the receiver. "Yes, Shauna?"

"Charity isn't feeling well. I've got my suspicions, but I'd feel better if you took a look at her."

"Oh dear." The older woman's voice reflected her concern. "I'll do that, but I'll go ahead and telephone her grandmother. Give me just a couple of minutes, and I'll come down to your room and pick her up."

"Thanks."

Shauna settled the other children down for a nap then scooped Charity into her arms. The little girl nuzzled against her shoulder.

"Mrs. Fritz is calling your grandma, honey. She's going to come and take you home." Even as she spoke the words, Shauna thought about Kent and wished she could call him herself to let him know. Maybe during her break she would do just that. Her heart quickened as she reflected on his situation. Single parents sure had their work cut out for them. She had to give him a lot of credit. *You should tell him that. Encourage him. Let him know what a good job he's doing.*

"I go home?" Charity rubbed at her arms, and Shauna tried to distract her.

"Yes. Soon."

"You come with me, teacher?"

Shauna's tried to hide her surprise. Did she really just say that? "I can't go with you, honey. I have to stay here and work."

Charity nuzzled a little closer. "I love you, teacher."

Shauna's heart swelled, and she embraced the toddler with a newfound joy. "I love you, too, honey."

Mrs. Fritz entered the room, a look of concern on her face. "How's our girl?"

"She's burning up." Shauna mouthed the words.

"I called her grandmother, but she's out of town on business. I tried her father, but he's out of the office. I'm trying to track down his cell number."

"I have it." Shauna shifted Charity's weight and reached for her cell phone.

"You do?" Mrs. Fritz's eyes reflected her curiosity.

Shauna took just a couple of moments to quietly explain her relationship with Kent Chapman—how they met, the things they had in common, and the things that divided them. She spoke in hushed tones so that she wouldn't wake Charity, who now dozed in her arms. Ultimately, Shauna had to confess, she found herself drawn to this man, though it defied all logic.

When she finished, Mrs. Fritz smiled. "Oh, Shauna," she said. "It must be wonderful to be young—to see your future with such clearly defined borders. Everything is so black and white."

"I thought it was. Now I'm not so sure."

"I have the benefit of many years behind me," Mrs. Fritz said. "And I can tell you, things don't always turn out like we think they're going to. No matter how carefully we lay out our plans, the Lord's plans for our lives are grander still. Sometimes, they're so far beyond our comprehension that we can't see them, even when they confront us at every turn."

"I know what you mean." Shauna held Charity a little closer and stroked her hair. "Sometimes we miss what's right in front of us." *Isn't that what Kent said that evening at the coffee shop? Didn't he say that people spend more time connecting with people they can't even see and ignore the ones they're with? Didn't he say that we should take advantage of the small moments and really connect with people?*

Mrs. Fritz's face widened into a broad smile. "Well, if I use my imagination, I can see some things quite clearly. For instance, I can see you happily married to a man like Kent Chapman, with a beautiful little girl like Charity to raise together. I can see your plans completely messed up, replaced with new and better plans. I can see all of that."

Shauna felt her cheeks flush. "I'm not sure what the Lord wants," she whispered. "I'm really not. I thought I had my life so carefully planned out—down to the last detail. But God apparently has other ideas. He's leading me in different directions. That's not easy for someone like me—someone who likes to have all their ducks in a row."

Mrs. Fritz chuckled. "I know you want to lead a well-planned, ordered life, honey. But how exciting to think the Lord trusts you enough to knock a few of those ducks out of the row. Makes for a great adventure."

"I just hope I'm up for it." Shauna sighed. "I thought I knew so much, and it turns out I'm clueless."

"Which means you're in a wonderful place of submission to the Lord. Don't you see? When we take our hands off of things, He's free to move. Maybe God has been waiting for you to admit that you're clueless so that He can clue you in."

Shauna smiled. "That's a funny way to look at it, but I'd be willing to bet you're right."

"Could be. Time will tell." Mrs. Fritz winked at her then moved in the direction of the door. "I could stand here and talk all day," she said, "But I'd better get back to the office and call Charity's Daddy."

"I go home?" Charity awoke with a start.

"Yes, honey." Shauna stroked the little girl's hair. "You're going home."

૨◆

Kent walked through the sanctuary, taking in the Christmas decorations.

"What do you think, Pastor Kent?" Delia Vasquez, one of the church's older parishioners, asked. "Did we do a nice enough job?"

He didn't answer for a moment, overwhelmed at the transformation. "I don't know how you did it," he said finally. "You ladies have outdone yourselves this year, Delia. Honestly. I don't know when I've ever seen anything more beautiful."

He couldn't help but notice her cheeks flush as she responded. "Thank you." She pointed to the back of the stage. "I particularly like the white lights against all of the greenery. Very classy."

"Very. And the Christmas tree looks better than ever. Did you make all of those bows yourself?"

She nodded. "Every last one."

"I'm sure the whole thing will be perfect for the Christmas program." He touched her shoulder gently. "I can't thank you enough. You work harder than most anyone I know."

She shrugged. "I figure it's just another way to tithe. I'm on social security, you know—so my financial giving is limited. But I can sure enough give of my time." Her face lit up in a broad smile.

"I wish everyone felt that way."

He looked around the room once more and couldn't help but think about Shauna. He hadn't seen her since Thanksgiving week, but he could almost picture her face as she looked around the sanctuary. "Not very twenty-first century," she might say. "Looks pretty traditional to me."

"Wait till you see our 3-D tree on the big screen," he might joke. "It's superimposed, but looks just like the real thing—only without all the work."

"Pastor?" Delia nudged him. "Thinking about Christmas?"

"I guess you could say that." He turned to face her. "I'm

excited about all of the activities, especially the candlelight service."

"I'm so happy to hear your sister will be joining us this year."

"Jessica and her husband Colin are driving in from Dallas to be here," Kent added. "Should be arriving any day now. I haven't seen her in months." *I wonder what Jessica would think about Shauna? Would she like her?*

"Jessica has the voice of an angel," Delia said. "I still remember how beautifully she sang 'O Holy Night' all those years. That girl is so gifted."

"Her husband is very good, too," Kent added. "He directs some of the larger performances at the Dallas Metropolitan Opera. God sure knew what He was doing when He paired those two up. You should hear them sing together. They're a perfect match—in every way. In fact, they're so much alike, it's remarkable."

"Funny how God works," Delia said with a goofy grin. "Bringing two people together like that. He did just the opposite in my case."

"What do you mean?"

"My husband and I were as different as night and day. If I said a thing was black, he'd argue it was white. If I wanted to live in the city, he'd rather settle in the country. Seemed like every time we turned around, we had to compromise. But that's what love is all about. I'm not sure I'd enjoy living with someone who agreed with me on every little thing. Might make for a pretty boring life."

Kent chuckled. "I understand. A little disagreement can be healthy, I suppose." His cell phone rang out, and he excused himself to answer it. "Hello?"

"Mr. Chapman?"

"Yes?"

"This is Mrs. Fritz up at the day care."

She sounded worried. Something must have happened to Charity. Kent's heart began to race as he asked, "Is everything okay?"

"I'm sorry to have to tell you this over the phone, Mr. Chapman, but it looks like Charity has the chicken pox."

"Are you sure?"

"Oh, I'm sure all right. She's covered in spots. I'm surprised you didn't notice them yourself."

Shame washed over Kent immediately. "To be honest, I did notice a few spots, but they looked like bites of some sort. We spent Saturday afternoon outside at the park, so I just figured. . ."

"I'm afraid you'll have to come and pick her up," Mrs. Fritz explained. "Chicken pox is highly contagious. We don't want to run the risk of infecting the other children."

"Of course." He glanced at his watch, trying to figure out how—and when—he could get away to pick her up. "I have a luncheon with twenty local pastors at noon," he explained, "and three private counseling sessions this afternoon. Maybe I could call my mother and. . ."

"I spoke to your mother just a few minutes ago. She's at some sort of a book festival in Austin."

"Oh, that's right." He bit his lip, trying to think of a solution. "Maybe I could come around 1:30 p.m. . ."

"I really think it would be best if you could come sooner," she argued. "Charity is miserable. She's been scratching all morning. She's here in my office with me, but really wants to go home with her daddy."

"Okay." He looked at his watch again. "I'll be there in fifteen minutes."

"Thank you. I know Charity will be happy to see you."

Mrs. Fritz signed off with a click, and Kent flew into action. He took three phone calls in the car—two from members of the congregation and one very encouraging call from Michael Kenner, one of the church's elders. He then telephoned his mother, letting her know about Charity's condition. Coincidentally, she and Andrew were already on the road, headed home from Austin.

When he walked through the front door of the day care, Charity rushed into his arms. "Daddy."

He held her tightly and whispered in her ear, "How's my girl?"

"I sick, Daddy." She clawed at her arms, and Kent pushed her sleeves up, gasping as he saw how irritated the little sores had become. He felt terrible for not noticing what should have been so obvious—more foolish still for not realizing she could have infected the other children.

Mrs. Fritz stood nearby with Charity's jacket in her hand. "I'm awfully glad you're here. She really needs her daddy today."

"Looks like it." He planted a kiss on her tiny cheek and slipped her jacket on, one arm at a time.

Out of the corner of his eye, Kent saw Shauna enter the large playroom to his right with her other students. He willed her to look his way. She glanced up, and their eyes met in a clear connection. A smile lit her face, and dimples appeared. Her beauty almost left him speechless. Kent waved, feeling more like one of the children than the grown man he was. Shauna waved in response and blew a kiss in Charity's direction.

Or was it his direction?

eighteen

Shauna knocked on the door of the unfamiliar house. Even from here, she could hear the sounds of voices raised in song coming from inside. A Christmas carol. She strained to listen. "O Holy Night." Apparently, no one heard her knocking, so she rang the bell, not just once, but twice.

Finally, Kent's mother answered the door. Her face lit up immediately, and she took Shauna by the hand at once.

"Shauna! How wonderful to see you again. Charity will be tickled pink." Mrs. Dougherty all but pulled Shauna into the living room. "Were you waiting long? We've been in here, singing our hearts out, getting ready for the Christmas program at church. Couldn't hear a thing."

Shauna pulled her hands from her jacket pockets and rubbed them together. "Not very long."

"You poor thing. I can tell you're shivering," Mrs. Dougherty shook her head. "Shame on me. Well, as soon as I make introductions, I'll get you a cup of coffee. It's brewing now. Sound good?"

"*Mmm*. Yes." Shauna looked around the beautiful living room, amazed at the family photos on every wall.

"My mother has turned this place into a shrine." A beautiful young woman with auburn hair rose from the piano bench and approached her. "We've asked her to stop taking pictures, but she's addicted to the camera."

"I love my family," Mrs. Dougherty said with a pout. "Nothing wrong with that."

"Nothing a twelve-step program wouldn't take care of, anyway." The young woman laughed, and Shauna couldn't help but join her.

"Where are my manners?" Shauna's grandmother exclaimed. "I need to make introductions. Shauna, this is my daughter, Jessica Phillips."

The lovely young woman extended her hand and Shauna shook it. "Nice to meet you."

"This is my husband, Colin." With a broad smile, Jessica gestured to the tall, dark-haired man still seated on the piano bench.

Colin stood and shook her hand, then sat in the large wing chair to her right.

Mrs. Dougherty's face lit up as she said, "Jessica and Colin sing with the Dallas Metropolitan Opera. You should hear them; they're amazing. In fact, they're singing together in the Christmas Eve candlelight service at church. You're going to be there, aren't you?"

"Well, I—I hadn't thought about it."

"You should come. I'm sure you'll love it. You just won't believe how wonderful they are."

"Mom," Jessica said with a look of consternation. "You don't need to give us such a glowing introduction. I'm sure that's not why Shauna came, to hear about us." She smiled broadly. "So, why did you come? To see my brother?" Jessica's eyes twinkled.

Shauna couldn't help but stammer. "Well, I—I. . .not exactly. I came to see Charity."

"Sugar and cream in your coffee?" Laura Dougherty called out as she headed toward the kitchen.

"Yes, please."

"So. . ." Jessica took her by the hand, "you're this teacher we've heard so much about. Charity talks about you all the time. Every time my brother calls, she gets on the phone and goes on and on about her school, her teacher, her friends."

Shauna nodded, her embarrassment almost getting the better of her. She had to wonder what sort of things the child might have said about her. "I'm sure she loves the school."

"What's not to love? And you—well, Kent has told me all about you." Jessica ushered her to the sofa and gestured for her to sit. "But he didn't tell me how pretty you were—just that you were awesome with kids and had a degree in early childhood education—those sorts of things."

"He—he told you that?"

"And more, but he'd probably die if he found out I told you." Jessica put her finger to her lips. "So maybe we'd better just stop there." She paused a moment then plunged forward. "But between you and me, we're all so excited to hear that he's actually going out there and meeting people. The fact that you two went on a couple of dates. . ."

Shauna felt her cheeks flush. Colin cleared his throat loudly from across the room, and Jessica took the hint.

"I'm sorry." Freckles lit her face as she whispered. "Not another word about all that. But after all Kent has been through, I'm just so happy to think. . ." Jessica's words faded away as Colin gave her an imploring look.

Shauna looked around the room, curious about Charity's whereabouts. "I was hoping to see Charity," she said. "How's she feeling?"

"I think she's a little better this afternoon," Jessica said. "And, if you can believe it, she's been napping. Don't have a clue how she slept through all the noise, but then again, she's a Chapman. We're pretty good at sleeping through anything."

At that very moment, Charity popped her head around the

corner. "Miss Shauna!" She raced to the sofa and jumped in Shauna's arms.

Shauna pulled her close and let the little girl wrap her in a warm embrace. "How are you feeling?"

"Itchy." Charity pulled up the arm of her flannel pajamas and showed off her spots, which were considerably larger and crustier than before.

Laura Dougherty entered the room with a cup of coffee in her hand. "No scratching, now." She set the cup on the coffee table in front of Shauna. "She's been rubbing at those spots all day long. I've covered them in calamine lotion—even gave her an oatmeal bath just before. But nothing seems to alleviate the itching. She just scratches like mad."

Charity hid her face in Shauna's shirt-sleeve. "I good girl."

"Sure you are." Jessica chuckled then shook her head. "She's something else, isn't she?"

"Yes." Shauna ran her fingers through Charity's hair, and the little girl relaxed in her arms. "She's something else." As she looked at the little doll in her snowman pajamas with loops of blond curls hanging in her eyes, Shauna recognized something anew. *This is a beautiful child. In fact, she's absolutely gorgeous.*

"Tell teacher what you want for Christmas, honey," Laura Dougherty said.

"I want a puppy!"

"You do?"

"It's all she talks about," Jessica said. "Puppy, puppy, puppy."

"What kind of puppy?" Shauna asked, gazing into the youngster's green eyes, which were lit with excitement.

"A pink puppy!"

"Pink?"

"I think she means red," Laura added quickly. "She always gets red and pink mixed up. But at any rate, she fell in love with a red dachshund we saw at the pet store last week."

"I can't wait to tell Kent." Jessica said. "Can't you see the look on his face now?" She laughed.

Shauna tried to imagine the look on Kent's face. What in the world would he do with a puppy? He could barely handle Charity. On the other hand, a puppy might be good for them both.

"I'll tell you what. . ." Shauna took Charity's hands and gave them a little squeeze. "I have a wonderful book about puppies at my house. I'll bring it to you so you can read it with your grandma. How about that?"

"You will?" Charity's eyes seemed to dance with joy.

"I will. But you have to promise something first."

"I promise! I promise!" Charity bounced up and down in her lap.

"You have to promise not to scratch your itchy spots." Shauna tried to muster up a serious face.

Charity sighed and didn't say anything for a moment. Finally, she gave a slow nod. "Okay. I no scratch."

"Good girl." Shauna held her close. "Good girl." And for the first time ever, Shauna contemplated the fact that Charity could very well turn out to be a good girl.

❧

Kent tapped his fingertips against the steering wheel as he sat in a sea of traffic on I-45 North. A cheerful holiday tune played on the radio, but he snapped it off, too concerned to be jolly at the moment.

For over an hour, he had tried to reach his mother but had been unsuccessful. Her house phone must be off the hook. Six times he dialed the number. Six times he had received a busy signal. Frustrated, he had even tried his mother's cell phone, only to get the answering machine.

Something must have happened to Charity. She hadn't felt well for the past couple days since her chicken pox diagnosis but had struggled through a particularly difficult time of it last night. Her temperature had spiked, and she spent all night tossing and turning.

"Mom probably took her back to the doctor," he reasoned aloud. Or worse. Maybe a trip to the emergency room. Maybe that's why her cell phone wasn't picking up. Maybe they were at the hospital now.

His mind immediately shifted back to that night—that awful night—when Faith never made it home. The call to come to the emergency room. The rushed drive there, not knowing what would await him once he arrived. Their last moments together as she clung to life. The fear that gripped his heart as she slipped away. The realization that he would be left alone to raise a daughter who needed a mother.

The anger at a God who would allow all of that to happen.

I can't go through that again. I can't. Though healing had eventually come, it had come with much wrestling and agonizing. How could he possibly make it through that sort of storm again?

Kent clutched the steering wheel a little tighter and prayed, "Lord, please protect Charity. And heal her, Father. Please." His heart twisted then released as the traffic cleared a bit. He quickly exited the freeway and scooted along the feeder road until he reached the turn-off for his mother's neighborhood.

He pulled up to the front of the house and gasped as he noticed the white Saturn in the driveway. *What in the world? Shauna?*

He leapt from the car and sprinted toward the front door. He stopped short when he heard singing coming from inside. A Christmas song. Someone played the piano with great gusto. *Jessica. She and Colin must be here. They'll know where Mom is.*

He opened the front door and stepped inside, completely unprepared for the scene inside the house. His sister sat at the piano, playing with fervor. Colin stood at her side, singing. His voice boomed across the place as if a microphone had been turned on. His mother sat in the recliner, merrily chiming in.

And Charity. . .

Charity sat on Shauna Alexander's lap on the sofa.

Kent didn't know whether to cry from sheer relief or chew them all out for not answering the phone. The music came to a grinding halt as soon as everyone realized he had joined them.

"Kent!" His sister stood and gave him a warm embrace. "It's good to see you again." She then whispered in his ear, "Why didn't you tell us how pretty she was?"

Kent felt his cheeks flush. "I'm so glad you made it safely." He gave her a peck on the cheek and whispered back, "Cut it out," then reached to shake his brother-in-law's hand. "Colin, thanks for coming on such short notice. Everyone at church is really looking forward to hearing you two sing this Sunday."

"Glad to do it."

"Daddy!" Charity ran to him and wrapped her tiny arms around his knees.

He scooped her into his arms and planted kisses on both cheeks. "How are you feeling?"

"I feel good." She grinned. "Miss Shauna come see me."

"I see that." He couldn't keep his lips from curling upwards as he looked at Shauna. His heart soared, and he fought to keep the joy from spilling out all over the room as he glanced at her left hand. *No ring.*

"I've been calling for over an hour." Kent looked around the room in the hopes someone would take responsibility.

"Really?" his mother asked. "I never heard the phone ring."

"It must be off the hook somewhere," he explained. "I just got a busy signal."

"I'll bet you're right." His mother left the room in search of the problem, only to return a few seconds later with the portable phone in her hand. "I found it under Charity's bed. She must have been trying to call someone."

"I call Daddy!" Charity exclaimed.

"Well, Daddy's here now." He stroked her cheek with the back of his hand.

"I love you, Daddy!" Charity ran back toward the sofa, crawled back up into Shauna's lap, and leaned her head against her shoulder. "I love teacher, too."

The room grew silent for a moment until Shauna gave her a light kiss on the cheek and responded, "I love you, too, Charity."

Kent struggled with the feeling of joy that suddenly washed over him. "Looks like she's feeling much better today," he observed.

"Must be all of the attention," Jessica said.

"She had a hard night last night." Kent spoke the words as much to Shauna as anyone in the room. "Really scared me."

"Teacher pray for me, Daddy," Charity snuggled her head against Shauna's arm.

"She did?" He couldn't help but smile at Shauna, but as he did, he felt every pair of eyes in the room bear down on him. "Looks like God answered her prayer." He took a seat on the couch next to Shauna and his daughter and tried to think of something to say. He found himself tongue-tied, unable to think straight.

"How are things at the school?" The words tumbled out.

"Oh, good," she explained. "We've been hanging Christmas decorations and getting ready for our little party in a few days.

We're sure missing Charity, though."

"Really?" He didn't mean the word as an accusation, but the look of pain in Shauna's eyes told him she had interpreted it as such.

"Of course," she said. "I sure hope she's able to come back in time for our Christmas party."

"She loves being at school." He gave her a comforting look. "Especially when you're there." He felt his cheeks grow warm. "And she always loves a party."

"So do I!" his mother exclaimed. "So why are we all sitting around gabbing? Let's get the music going again. Come on, everyone. Let's sing some Christmas carols."

Jessica sprang up from her seat and headed to the piano. As "Jingle Bells" began to spring forth from her fingers, the room came alive with Christmas cheer. All of Kent's earlier fears were washed away as he joined in the song—all of the people he loved best at his side.

nineteen

Kent looked over the congregation from his seat on the platform. If this evening's service got any better, he might just bust a few buttons. Already, the choir had performed a beautiful Christmas medley, then joined with the congregation to sing several of their favorite carols together. Jessica and Colin combined their skilled voices for a unique version of "What Child is This?" The song seemed an appropriate choice in light of Jessica's news just this morning that she and Colin were expecting their first child come summer.

Kent's heart could hardly contain the joy. But he had to stay focused. The evening would be drawing to a close soon, and he didn't want to miss his favorite part. Any second now the music for "O Holy Night" would begin, and all of the memories of past Christmases would fade together into a beautiful new picture of holiday hope and joy.

His heart warmed when the familiar introduction began. Several of the teens from the congregation came forward as they had been instructed. They traveled in silence from pew to pew, handing out the small white candles that would soon light the room. Jessica's voice rang out above the crowd, clear and strong. "O holy night, the stars are brightly shining. . . ."

Kent looked out over his congregation, the words stirring him as never before. He felt a mixture of joy and sorrow, knowing his time as interim pastor would soon be drawing to a close. The board had only asked him to stay through the end of the year, after all. Though the interview process had moved at a snail's pace, he felt sure they must have made some decision in recent days.

They must be coming closer to finding the right man for the job. That had to be the reason they had asked him to stay after tonight's service for a brief meeting. He had noticed both a sense of excitement and peace in the countenances of those involved in the process. Soon he would receive the news that would release him from this position—and send him in search of another.

Thank You for this time in my life, Lord. Thank You for trusting me and for allowing me such an amazing opportunity. I know I'm young, but I feel like I've gained several years' worth of knowledge in such a short time.

Had it only been months?

Jessica sang on, her voice like that of an angel. Kent looked out at those in attendance, amazed to see so many new faces. At least twenty or thirty new members had joined them during his brief stay behind the pulpit. Many more were yet to come; he felt sure of it. His mind reeled as he considered all of the things the church could do on the evangelism front over the next months and years. His imagination almost got the better of him before he realized these were not his decisions. At least, they wouldn't be for long.

But oh, how great it had been to come up with ideas to help the church grow and flourish. What a wonderful time he had had! Kent had loved getting to know the new people but had really enjoyed spending time with the more established folks, as well.

And then there were those who had been in limbo. One in particular. Kent couldn't help but smile as his gaze came to rest on Josh Ebert, who sat in the third row with his wife and boys. The reports, at least so far, had all been good. Josh seemed to be on the mend, and Vicky's face—and attitude—reflected a new sense of hope. Their young sons sat between them, faces awash with contentment.

That's what this season is all about, isn't it? Hope. Contentment. Restoration. Kent's heart swelled. *Yes, not just for others, but for me, as well.*

The last two Christmases had been the most difficult of his life, Kent had to admit, but this one felt different in so many ways.

"New. I've made all things new."

And You've done a work in my heart I could never have imagined. You've healed from the pain of the past and given me a hope for the future.

Kent stood and made his way to the podium. Once there, he gave the instructions to light the candles. One by one the room came alive with light—starting with a soft glow and growing into a shimmer that took his breath away. By the time the final candle came alive, light flooded the whole place.

"The stars are brightly shining." As the words to Jessica's song echoed in his ears, Kent couldn't help but think each and every member of Grace Community Church was a star all its own. And yet, each person was more valuable, more precious than a million stars. *Let every light keep burning, Lord. Don't let even one go out.*

His gaze settled on a group of people in the third row—his own little galaxy. His mother and stepfather sat side-by-side, taking turns holding Charity, who squirmed as much or more than ever.

And then there was the young woman seated to his mother's left. With the soft glow of the candlelight flickering in front of Shauna Alexander's face, her beauty lit a flame in his heart that he could no longer deny. He would not fight to put it out. Instead, he would embrace it as never before.

 *

Shauna brushed away loose tears as Jessica's song ended. She couldn't help but whisper the word *beautiful* as she dabbed at her eyes.

Beautiful service, beautiful song, a beautiful family seated all around her—and a man so used by God standing at the podium that she had to confess his beauty, as well. *I have to tell him. I need to let him know how proud I am of all he has accomplished in this place. And I have to let him know something else, too.*

I have to let him know that I'm falling in love with him.

The musicians began to play "Silent Night," and the congregation rose as one. The words, sweet and simple, brought fresh tears to her eyes. "All is calm, all is bright." She could hardly sing past the lump in her throat.

"I still speak in the stillness, in the calm."

"Round yon virgin mother and Child." She whispered the words, unable to get them out. *Yes, Lord. I hear Your voice.*

"Don't doubt the call I've placed on your life to work with children. There will be many of them in your life. They need your love."

I'm so inadequate, Father.

"Sleep in heavenly peace." The congregation continued on with the soothing lullaby, and Shauna closed her eyes to focus.

"Peace, child. My strength is made perfect in you."

Charity tapped on Shauna's leg, startling her back to reality. "Teacher?"

Shauna looked down at the youngster. "What is it, honey?" she whispered.

"I hold candle?" Charity's lips formed a familiar pout.

"Well. . ." Shauna looked up at Laura Dougherty for some show of support but found the other woman stood with her eyes closed, clearly enjoying the music.

"Maybe we can hold it together," Shauna whispered. She sat down on the pew, and Charity crawled up into the spot next to her. With her own hands very carefully holding the candle, she allowed Charity to slip her tiny fingers around the edges of the bottom.

With both hands now firmly holding the little light in place, Charity sang aloud with a voice as clear as an angel's. Her breath caused the candle to flicker, and her precious voice brought a smile to Shauna's face—a smile quickly replaced with tears of great joy. They came slowly at first and then with greater intensity.

Charity nuzzled up against her and whispered the words, "I love you, teacher," so softly that Shauna had to ask her to repeat them. When she finally heard—and fully understood—the youngster's heartfelt offering, Shauna's heart felt as if it would explode with joy. In one night's time she had discovered her heart was capable of not only love for a man. . .but the purest of love for his daughter, as well.

❧

Kent emerged from the meeting, amazed to find the church nearly empty. He finally located his mother and Charity in the back of the sanctuary, but most of the others had apparently already gone.

Please, Lord. Don't let Shauna be gone. I need to talk to her.

"How did it go?" His mother yawned as she stood from the pew.

"Fine, fine." *I'll have to fill her in later.*

"You were sure in there long enough."

"We were?" Kent looked down at his watch, shocked to discover almost an hour had passed. "That's odd. Felt like just minutes."

"We still have some last-minute things to take care of at home," his mother whispered. "For you-know-who." She pointed down at his daughter, who slept soundly on the pew.

"Christmas morning," he gasped. "I got so caught up in everything going on up here that I almost forgot."

His mother chuckled. "Trust me, she won't let you forget."

As he reached down to scoop Charity into his arms, he asked his mother the question that had weighed on his heart. "Is, uh. . .is Shauna gone?"

His mom nodded. "She stayed for a half hour or so but had to get home. She needs to spend time with her family on Christmas Eve."

"I understand." He did, but he also understood that his heart might explode if he didn't share its contents with her soon.

"She really enjoyed the service tonight, honey." Kent's mother patted him on the back as they made their way out into the foyer.

"Really?"

"Yes. We had a long talk afterwards. She wants to make this her church home."

"I'm glad. I want that, too."

"I believe you want more than that." His mother's eyes twinkled as she added, "What you're wanting might make for a great Christmas present. The very best."

"Maybe." Kent shrugged and tried his best to hide the smile that wanted to spread so wide his cheeks would split. "But everything in its time."

"Fine. No more from me on this subject," she said with a wink. "At least for now."

As they walked out into the parking lot, Kent's mind reeled. He couldn't possibly bother Shauna anymore tonight. Should he call her on Christmas Day and disturb her family time?

Probably not. But when would he see her again? When could he tell her?

"Oh!" His mother turned to him rather abruptly as he reached his car. "I forgot to ask you how the meeting went. Is everything okay?"

He didn't respond for a moment as he debated whether or not to tell her what the board members had decided. Finally, he settled on a brief answer. "Yes. Everything went fine."

"You're not telling me much." She gave him an inquisitive look.

"No, I'm not. We can talk about it later, okay? It's late, and I need to get Charity into bed."

"Okay. But I doubt I'll get much sleep tonight, then. It's not nice to make an old woman worry."

Kent chuckled, understanding her ploy to get more information from him. "You're not old, Mom. And I certainly don't want to worry you."

His mother climbed into her car and started the engine. She pulled away and waved with a mischievous grin.

Kent shivered against the cold as he strapped Charity into her car seat. She awoke for just a moment then promptly fell asleep again. As he settled into the driver's seat, Kent reflected on his mother's curiosity. Her eyes had been full of questions, but Kent couldn't bring himself to give answers.

At least not yet.

twenty

At 3:15 a.m. Kent sat at his computer, trying to compose a poem. The idea had come to him after crawling into bed at two. *I don't have a present for Shauna. What can I give her?* He had struggled with the question for over an hour before he climbed out of bed and dragged himself to the computer.

"I'm not very good at putting things down on paper." Had he really said those words to Shauna as they stood in front of the computer store? What, then, would compel him to think he might now be able to compose a poem, of all things?

And yet, the idea wouldn't leave him alone. His heart might very well erupt from his chest if he didn't get these feelings out. And the sooner, the better. He typed a few words then backspaced with a rapid *tap, tap, tap* to get rid of the nonsense. Once again, he tried and, once again, he ended up wiping all of it away.

"How can I begin to tell her in one poem what I can't even formulate in my head?" he mumbled. "None of this makes sense to me, and if it doesn't make sense to me, it sure won't to her." And yet he must say something. Otherwise, he might never sleep again.

After a few moments of prayer and introspection, Kent began to type once more.

> *How can I begin to send*
> *A message I can't comprehend?*
> *Mere words could simply not convey*

> *My heart's true hopes or dreams today.*
> *When your lovely face appears*
>   *This coward turns away in fear.*
> *If courage would rise up in me*
>   *My heart could surely speak its piece.*
> *And so I send with Christmas cheer*
>   *This message, cryptic and unclear*
> *For if I did reveal my mind*
>   *You might, within, the real truth find.*

He stared at the page, trying to figure out a title. The words, "Cryptic Message" seemed to type themselves at the top of the document. Now to figure out how to sign the silly thing. "With love?" "Cordially?" "Sincerely?" He settled on, "In Christ's love, Kent Chapman."

With a click, he sent the document out, out, out—across the Internet and into her waiting inbox. He leaned back against his chair, wishing, for a moment, he could take it back, wishing he could unsend it.

Just as quickly, he thanked God for giving him the courage to press the SEND button. Only one problem remained—how to breathe until she responded.

ॐ

Shauna awoke on Christmas morning with a peace she hadn't felt in years. This overwhelming sense of peace intermingled with a heady joy as she contemplated her newly discovered feelings for Kent Chapman. What an amazing Christmas gift— to experience love, real love. And how wonderful to imagine the Christ of Christmas might be so loving and gracious as to give her the desires of her heart.

Shauna's spirit carried the songs of the night before. The words ran over and over in her mind, and she felt truly free in her spirit.

"All is calm, all is bright." Yes, everything did seem calmer today. And her thoughts were crystal clear. She had fallen in love with Kent Chapman—not just the "Twenty-first Century Pastor," not just the father of a precocious little girl—but the man. And once the presents were opened and dinner eaten, she would find a way to let him know. Surely he felt the same. Otherwise, the Lord would not have given her such a peace.

The morning moved on much as their Christmases past. She and her parents opened presents together after reading the Christmas story from the Bible—tradition they had begun when she was a little girl. Then her aunts, uncles, and cousins began to arrive.

With a houseful of people to contend with, she had little time to think about what she would say to Kent when the opportunity afforded itself. But later that afternoon, as the crowd dwindled down, Shauna headed off to the computer, convinced she could no longer put off the inevitable. She must compose a letter to Kent Chapman. What she had to say could best be said on paper. If she tried to speak the words in person, she would likely stumble all over herself.

Her computer booted up properly. She signed online and tried to open an e-mail. Right away, the computer locked up and would not function at all. Frustrated, she shut the system down and rebooted. Immediately, the virus scanner picked up a problem. She let the software scan the machine, horrified to discover a virus from the suspect e-mail. The words *Cryptic Message* appeared in the subject box, but the rest had been scrambled. The whole thing looked like nothing but gibberish. Had someone tried to sabotage her computer? A hacker, perhaps?

Shauna quarantined the virus, but still the problem persisted. The machine continued to lock up, finally freezing altogether.

Two more times she shut down the computer and rebooted, but never made it past the front screen without everything coming to a standstill.

Disappointed, she turned the computer off for the last time. Now what? Should she call Kent? Then again, how could she disturb him on Christmas? He would be spending the day with family. And, come to think of it, that's probably what she should be doing right now, as well.

Shauna headed back out into the living room and joined her mother and father for a quiet conversation in front of the fireplace. They told stories of Christmases gone by and laughed at a few of the presents their relatives had brought. They nibbled at pieces of pie and sipped cups of hot chocolate. Her father eventually dozed off in his chair, and her mother picked up a book to read.

As drowsiness set in, Shauna stumbled into bed for a long, well-deserved nap. She didn't bother changing into nightclothes, convinced she would only close her eyes for a few glorious minutes.

She awoke to sunlight streaming through the window. Groggy and confused, she rubbed at her eyes. Her gaze shifted to the alarm clock, and she nearly came out of her skin.

"You've got to be kidding me." She sat up in the bed as she realized the clock read 6:25 a.m. "I slept through the night? No way!" She sprang from the bed and flew into action. Thirty-five minutes later she arrived at the day care, eyes still heavy from sleep and heart still heavy from not speaking to Kent.

❧

On the morning after Christmas, Kent could no longer contain himself. He signed onto the computer and checked his e-mail. He didn't find a letter or a response of any kind from Shauna. His chest tightened as he realized she must have read his poem and ignored it altogether. Maybe she sat at her computer this very minute, trying to compose a "thanks-but-no-thanks" letter. Kent let his imagination run wild, nearly making himself sick over the whole thing—sicker still as he checked his other e-mails.

Just when he thought things couldn't possibly get any worse, Kent discovered a message in his inbox from Shauna's Internet provider. According to the note, he had somehow sent Shauna's computer a virus—and not just any virus, but the latest, most volatile one to date.

Kent scratched his head, trying to make sense of all of this. How in the world could he have contaminated her computer when his machine was virus-free? He ran his scanner and quickly discovered the problem. A random junk e-mail he had opened briefly on Christmas Eve night had apparently been infected with the potent bug. Kent tossed the e-mail, but the virus had remained, worming its way onto his hard drive. Without knowing it, he had inadvertently contaminated not just his own computer, but hers, as well.

Horrified, Kent struggled to figure out what to do. He tried to quarantine the virus, but the crazy thing seemed to have a mind of its own. The computer screen began to flash and he couldn't seem to control the mouse. He tried shutting down and rebooting, but that didn't seem to accomplish anything. The problem persisted. With the screen bouncing all over the place, he stood and considered his options.

I could reformat the hard drive and start over, but then I'd lose all of my files. Or maybe I could quickly back up the files, even though the computer is acting up. Maybe it's not too late.

He attempted to do so but met with problem after problem. By the time he finished fighting with the machine, Kent had to conclude the obvious. There was nothing he could do.

Not only had he lost the opportunity to share his heart with Shauna, he might very well have lost all of his sermon notes and personal files, as well. Taking the computer back to the repair shop appeared to be the only solution. Surely they would know what to do.

twenty-one

The following afternoon, Kent pulled into the parking lot of Computers Unlimited. He glanced at his watch and whispered a prayer that the store would still be open. 4:59 p.m. Surely someone would still be here.

If only his meeting at church hadn't lasted so long, he might have gotten off to an earlier start. If only he had remembered to put gas in his car this morning, he might not have had to stop minutes ago. And if only he could stop thinking about Shauna Alexander every waking moment, he might then remember how to do the everyday things like eat, sleep, and breathe.

Kent walked to the back of his car and opened the trunk, then gave the computer a hard stare. *I ought to toss the crazy machine into the nearest dumpster and buy a new laptop.* If not for the files he needed to save, he would do just that. Instead, he scooped the PC up into his arms and closed the trunk with his elbow. He made it to the door just as Bill Conner, the store manager, reached to lock it.

"Please?" Kent mouthed the word through the glass.

Bill nodded and opened the door. In less than a minute, Kent explained the problem and handed the machine over once again. Mr. Conner tagged the PC and promised this time he would not send it home with the wrong owner. Kent couldn't help but chuckle. The laughter relaxed him a little, and he was reminded that nothing—not even the breakdown of his computer—could spoil this day unless he let it.

And the day was far from over. With the machine safely handed off, he must head home through evening traffic, have dinner with his daughter, and then do the one thing he had been terrified to do since Christmas Eve—call Shauna Alexander.

Kent walked back out to the parking lot, unable to shake the feeling that something was wrong. As he approached the car, the horrible moment of revelation came. "My keys." They weren't in his pocket. He scrambled to check the other pocket. Nothing.

He sprinted back to the store, rapping on the door. The frustrated store manager opened it once again, and Kent apologized then began a frantic search for the keys.

"When was the last time you saw them?" Mr. Conner asked as he joined in the search.

"Um. . ." Kent thought about that for a minute. "I used them to open the trunk."

"And then?"

"And then I. . ." Kent groaned as he realized what must have happened. "I'll bet I set them down inside the trunk when I went to pick up the computer. And then I. . ." *I closed the trunk with my elbow. I remember. The keys are locked in the trunk.* He slapped himself in the head and leaned against the counter.

Mr. Conner's expression softened. "Do you need to use my phone to call someone? I don't mind." He gestured toward the phone on the counter near the register.

"I guess so." Kent quickly dialed his mother's number, praying she would answer quickly. Only when the answering machine picked up did he remember she and Andrew had prior plans to go out to dinner with old friends. He needed to pick up Charity from the day care—and quickly.

"I need to call a locksmith," he said. "Do you have a phonebook?"

"I think I've got one in the back. I'll go check."

Kent tried to reason things out in his head as he glanced at his watch. 5:14 p.m. That meant he had exactly forty-six minutes to get his car open, drive to the day care, and pick up Charity. If everything went well, he could still make it. Of course, nothing today had gone particularly well.

I should call Mrs. Fritz, just in case. As he reached for the phone, a loud rap on the front door caught his attention. He turned just in time to see Shauna Alexander's beautiful face staring at him through the glass. With the joy that rose up inside him, Kent had to confess she might very well have been an angel.

&

The hefty PC very nearly slipped through Shauna's hands as she stared through the glass at Kent Chapman. The shock of finding him here so unexpectedly sent her heart reeling and her hands trembling. She looked again, just to make sure. *Yep. It's him.*

For the last twenty-four hours she had tried to work up the courage to call Kent, tried to pray about her growing feelings. And for two days the Lord had been silent.

Is this Your answer, Father?

For a moment, neither of them moved. It was as if they were both frozen in time and space.

Finally Kent flew into action. He sprinted to the door and pushed it open. "You're here." He took the computer out of her arms.

"*You're* here." Shauna stared in silence at Kent, unable to formulate even one sensible word beyond that opening statement.

He gave her a wink as he spoke. "We've got to stop meeting like this."

The smile that lit his face sent her heart soaring. "Doesn't look like *we* have anything to do with it." *Lord, this is You. You've arranged this, just like You arranged our meeting that very first time.*

"I don't believe in coincidence." Kent's green eyes narrowed as he grew more serious. "I believe there are God-incidents, and this certainly ranks up there with some of the best I've been privileged to witness first-hand."

"Me, too." She couldn't seem to control her smile.

Bill Conner approached from the back of the store. He looked surprised to see her. "Why. . .hello there. It's Ms. Alexander, isn't it?"

"Yes."

"Let me guess." He stared at her computer then shook his head in disbelief. "I don't know what to make of the two of you. Are you sure you're not doing this on purpose?" Just about the time Shauna opened her mouth to deny such a humorous accusation, Mr. Conner turned his attentions to Kent. "I looked everywhere for a phone book but couldn't find one. You're welcome to call information."

"Thanks, but I think my problem's just been solved." Kent nodded in Shauna's direction, and she had to wonder what he meant. "At least, I hope so. Could you give me a ride up to the day care? I need to pick up Charity."

He explained his predicament with the car, and she had to chuckle. "Sounds like my day." She handed off her computer to a somewhat-frustrated store manager, and they were on their way across the parking lot.

As they settled into the front seat of her car, Kent blurted out, "I gave you a virus."

"What?" She paused to absorb his words. "Are you talking about my computer, or is there something else I should be concerned about?"

"Your computer." He stared at her intently, and her cheeks warmed. "I didn't mean to do it."

She put the key in the ignition and turned on the car. "So what happened? Was it just a fluke?"

"Yes. I meant to give you something else."

Now his cheeks reddened, and Shauna had to wonder at the merriment in his eyes. He pulled a piece of paper out of his pocket.

"What in the world?" She watched as he grew more nervous by the minute.

He pressed the crumpled sheet of paper into her palm, and she slowly unfolded it. "Cryptic message." She looked up into his eyes, not understanding. "I'm confused."

"I was, too." He flashed a broad smile. "But I'm better now. I printed this up on Christmas Eve. It's the only copy I have. The original was responsible for destroying your computer."

"Wow." Her eyes widened. "Must be pretty potent. So what is it?"

"Take a look."

She scanned the words, startled to find a poem, clearly penned by Kent himself. She tried to make sense of the words, tried to imagine that he really meant them in the way she now wanted to take them. Truly, there was no other way to read it. He cared for her and had been afraid to tell her.

Shauna looked into his eyes and tapped her fingers on her lips. "You wrote this for me?"

"Yes." His gaze shifted downward, and she sensed his embarrassment.

"On Christmas Eve?"

"Yes." He leaned a bit closer, and she could feel her pulse in her ears.

"I—I. . ."

"I've wanted to talk to you for days, but I was so scared," he explained. "The poem was. . .my goofy attempt to get your attention."

"No," she argued, fighting the urge to kiss him right there, on the spot. "It's not goofy. And you've certainly got my attention now."

"I wanted to come up with something really amazing to tell you how I feel—how I've felt for a while now." He paused to give her a winsome look. "But remember, I've never been very good at putting things on paper."

"You did say that." Shauna couldn't help but smile. "In this very parking lot, if memory serves me correctly."

He nodded. "That's right. We were here, weren't we?"

"It seems a lot of firsts have taken place in this parking lot." Shauna's heart overflowed with joy as she looked into his eyes. "The first time we met. The first computer fiasco. The first time we talked about church things. The first time you told me you were a 'Twenty-first Century Pastor.' " She paused for a moment, praying he would read her heart.

"Ah."

"The first time we talked about our personal computer files," she continued on. "The first time we talked about the weather."

"I remember." Kent stared intently into her eyes and then gently leaned forward as if he had some great secret to tell. "But you missed one," he whispered.

"Did I?" She spoke softly as she felt his breath warm against her cheek.

"You did." With the tip of his index finger, he traced her cheek. And then, just as she prayed it would happen, their lips met in the sweetest kiss she had ever known.

Another first.

twenty-two

Three weeks after Christmas, Shauna joined Kent's family at a local pizza parlor to celebrate Charity's third birthday. The room came alive with activity as nearly a dozen of her students from the day care filled the place. Their parents joined the fray, making for a chaotic scene, but certainly nothing she hadn't grown used to in her months at the school.

In fact, she had to admit, growing to love and understand a room full of two-year-olds had certainly opened her eyes to a whole new world of possibilities. And coincidentally, most of the children seemed to be changing right before her eyes. Many had already outgrown the terrible twos and appeared to be moving into a new phase—one she liked to call the "inquisitive threes."

In particular, she couldn't help but notice how much Charity had changed over the past few months. *Lord, has she changed, or am I the one? Have I softened in my attitude toward her?* The idea wouldn't leave her mind.

Shauna looked out across the room and tried to keep an eye on all of them at once.

"You can relax." Kent gave her a quick peck on the cheek. "No need to play teacher today. You're not at school. And besides, their parents are all here."

"Just habit, I guess." Shauna shrugged and turned her attentions to Kent. She leaned her head on his shoulder and thanked God for all He had done in her life in such a short time. *You knew what You were up to, Father. And I'm so grateful.*

After a quick head count, she and Kent ordered enough pizza to feed an army, then sent the kids off to play. She leaned against him, and he slipped his arm around her shoulder.

"Having fun?" he asked.

She nodded, happier that she had been in ages.

"Looks like our parents are getting along." She pointed to the table where the two older couples sat chatting like lifelong friends.

"It's great, isn't it?" He reached to plant a soft kiss in her hair. "Our families are coming together."

Her heart swelled, and she thought for a moment she might cry. Instead, she forced herself to stay focused on the children. "I'm so glad." *We really are one happy family. And I can see my life like this. Forever.* She forced down the lump in her throat as the idea magnified itself. *I could marry this man. I could live like this forever.*

She and Kent joined their parents at the table, keeping a close eye on the children from their seats. She marveled at the joy in Kent's eyes and wondered if she looked as deliriously happy.

"Hey, you two." Her mother looked up with a smile. "Have a seat."

They sat and visited with their parents. Her father dove into an old story about life in the military, and Kent's parents listened intently. Kent's mom shared a little bit about her rocky journey in the years following her husband's untimely death, and they concluded that the Lord had, indeed, managed to bring joy into a sorrowful situation.

All the while, the children played. Charity's squeals of joy could be heard above the others, but at least they were happy squeals. At one point, little Dinah ran over to let them know that Clay was lost. Shauna sprang from her chair and raced to the child's mother, who had just discovered him hiding in the balls. He dove in again squealing with laughter.

The pizza arrived, and all of the women worked together to get the children settled down. Charity sat at the head of the table, chattering merrily with her friends as she ate. Shauna took it all in with a smile. She watched Charity from a distance, noting how social she seemed, and how quiet, in comparison to the child she knew just a few short months ago.

After the pizza, Kent stood and addressed the room. "Let's all sing." He started a rousing chorus of "Happy Birthday," and Charity's cheeks blazed with excitement.

"Cake, Daddy!" She bounced up and down in her chair. "I eat my princess cake."

Kent's mother pulled a beautiful cake out of the box, and all of the children hollered with delight.

"Pretty, pretty!" Abigail squealed.

Bobby reached out to stick his fingers in the frosting, but his mother quickly pulled his hand away. Pieces of cake were cut and handed out, and Shauna chuckled as she watched the children dive into the frosting, most ignoring the cake altogether. She leaned back in her chair and smiled as the scene continued to unfold. With her parents, her students, and the man she loved all together in one room, she truly felt she could face the new year with renewed hope and excitement.

&a

Kent stood and surveyed the group, his heart full of joy. *How many years has it been since I've felt like this, Lord? How many?* Truly God had restored his heart and his hope for a future—a really good thing, considering all the work that lay ahead in raising his daughter.

But at least, Lord willing, he wouldn't have to do it alone. Kent glanced down at Shauna. Her face, almost as cherublike and innocent as the children's, shone like a star in this sky—a star in his sky, anyway. He didn't know if he could put into words the feelings that swept across his heart as he watched her now, though he had gotten a little better at putting words on paper in the past few weeks. With his new full-time position as pastor at Grace Community Church, there would be many more sermons in the future, many more times to share his heart.

Your blessings are without end, Father. How can I begin to thank You? You are truly a God of new beginnings.

His heart pounded in anticipation as he remembered the task ahead. If he ever needed the Lord's help, this would be the time.

"Now comes the fun part." Kent leaned down to whisper in Shauna's ear. He turned his attention to the group and announced, "It's time for presents!"

The squealing began in earnest now. Parents held their children tightly, trying to bring a sense of order.

"My birthday!" Danny hollered. "My birthday."

His mother shushed him right away.

Charity clapped her hands in excitement. "My birthday. I three years old!" She held up three chubby fingers with dedicated zeal.

Yes, you are three years old, and I can hardly believe it. It seems just yesterday you were born; just yesterday you took your first little steps. And now. . .

Kent shook his head in disbelief as he stared at the little girl in front of him. No longer a baby, she had truly grown into a lovely child. Her blond curls had grown quite long, and her eyes sparkled with joy as she reached for her first present.

Kent tried to keep his wits about him. *Don't forget what you're doing.*

One by one, the presents were opened. Charity squealed with glee as she opened a box with a princess crown and slippers inside. "I a princess!"

"Yes you are, honey." Kent's mother gave her a kiss on the cheek. "You're our little princess."

The children squealed as she opened the next gift, a sand art kit. Then came a beautiful dress from Shauna's parents and multiple other toys from the children at the day care. Finally, Shauna slipped a carefully wrapped box in his daughter's direction. He had to wonder what she might have selected; such secrecy had surrounded its choosing.

Charity's jaw lowered in amazement as she discovered the beautiful pink ballet outfit inside the box.

"Miss Shauna, I love you!" She held up the pink leotard and package of tights, then grabbed the tiny pink ballet shoes and clutched them to her chest. "I dance! I dance!"

"How did you know?" Kent leaned down to whisper in Shauna's ear.

"I've been paying attention." Shauna smiled. "But that's not all. I have one more surprise." She reached to pull a gift bag out from under the table. Charity yanked the tissue paper out and hollered out as she lifted out the pink tutu. "Pretty!"

Shauna stood and approached Charity. "I know you want to dance, honey," she said. "And I thought you might like this. Maybe one day soon you can dance for us."

"I dance now!" Charity jumped from her seat, and it took all of Kent's wisdom to get her seated once again. His heart nearly burst as he looked at Shauna—his Shauna. This move on her part was the icing on the cake, no pun intended. In some ways, it sealed the deal.

"I have one more present," he announced to the group. "But it's for someone else at the table."

The children all began to scream at once. "Me! Me! I want present!"

Kent shook his head and pulled the little box from his pocket. For nearly two hours he had guarded it with great care. Now, finally, he could release it to its rightful owner. He turned to face Shauna, who looked a bit perplexed.

"I have a present for Miss Shauna." He spoke pointedly for the benefit of the children. "But I have to ask her a question first."

As he dropped to one knee, Kent's pulse sang in his ears. *This is the moment I've prayed about.*

Shauna's face reddened immediately, and her hands covered her mouth as the truth registered. "Kent?"

"Shauna. . ." His voice trembled then steadied. "I want to start by telling you what an amazing gift you have been to me and Charity these past few months. We've both fallen in love with you."

At this, a couple of the children giggled. Clay slapped himself in the head and groaned.

Shauna's smiled widened, and Kent forced himself to stay focused. "I would be so honored"—he swallowed hard—"if you would make me the happiest man on the earth by becoming my wife. Will you marry me, Shauna?"

His gaze locked into hers, and his pulse raced so quickly, Kent thought for a moment he might pass out. She nodded, slowly at first, then with zeal. Tears rushed down her cheeks, and her hand shook in his as he slipped the ring on her finger. All around the table, people began to clap. Shauna sprang to her feet and threw her arms around his neck, locking him in an embrace.

"How did you manage to pull this off?" she whispered in his ear.

"I had a little help." He gestured to their parents, and her cheeks reddened once again. She looked at her mother in shock. "You knew about this?"

Mrs. Alexander nodded. "Sure did."

"And you?" Shauna looked at his mother, amazement sweeping over her like a flood.

"Yep." Laura Dougherty flashed a broad smile.

Shauna looked down at her finger then back up at Kent. "I'm so happy, I just don't know what to say."

"Hey now, I thought I was the one who struggled to come up with the right thing to say." He wrapped her in his arms.

"You're great with words," she reminded him. "Remember that awesome poem you wrote me?"

Kent groaned. "That was awful."

"No." She looked at him with great seriousness. "It was beautiful. And you know what else is beautiful?"

"What?"

"*She* is." Shauna pointed down to the end of the table, where Charity sat eating her piece of cake. "Our daughter."

Our daughter. Kent's eyes filled up nearly as quickly as the idea registered fully. Charity would soon have a mother. And he would soon have a wife.

epilogue

"How are you feeling, Son?" Kent looked up as he heard his mother's voice.

"I'm great." In fact, he didn't remember ever feeling more joy or peace.

"Where are all those groomsmen of yours? Did they chicken out?" She looked around the room.

"I have a sneaking suspicion they snuck out to sabotage my car." Kent looked at his watch. "They made a commitment to be back in the room in five minutes." He fumbled with his necktie, but nerves got the better of him. He couldn't seem to get it straight, no matter how many times he tried.

His mother came closer to help him out. "I just came from seeing Shauna."

"You did?" His heart felt as if it had elevated into his throat. "How is she? Is she nervous? What does she look like? I'm sure she's beautiful."

"Whoa, whoa!" His mother laughed. "Too many questions. And I'm not giving away a thing. You'll discover all of the answers yourself in just a few minutes."

Kent sighed. "Okay."

She continued to work on his tie as she spoke. "You should hear all of the conversations going on out in the sanctuary."

"Are there a lot of people?"

His mother smiled. "I think you're going to be stunned. The place is packed out. And they're still coming in, if you can believe it." She continued to maneuver his tie as she spoke.

"Really?" Kent looked at his watch. "It's only a quarter till three. We don't start for fifteen minutes."

His mother shrugged. "I know. But they all are entertaining themselves by watching that photo slide presentation you and Shauna put together on the overhead projection screen. I've never heard so many chuckles, especially when they saw that picture of you in first grade with no teeth." His mother stepped back to examine the tie then untied it and began again.

Kent groaned. "I didn't want to use that picture, but Shauna insisted. She thought it was cute."

"It is," his mother agreed. "You were adorable then, and you're adorable now." She gave him a pat on the shoulder.

"I thought you said I was a tough case as a kid," he reminded her.

"True." She spoke with a hint of laughter in her voice. "But time has affected my memory."

Her words struck a chord. "Time has affected my memory, too," he had to confess. "My painful memories of losing Faith are fading. New memories are taking their place. I'm so grateful for that. I don't ever want to forget Faith—and I'm sure I never will—but I'm happy to forget the pain. I really think the worst is behind me now. I feel like I can look to the future without that"—he stumbled a bit over the words—"without that lump in my throat. You know?"

"I do know." His mother reached to hug his neck then spoke with tears in her eyes. "I can't help but think that time is a part of God's plan to extend mercy to His children. How else could we walk through such stormy times and still come out on the other side with so few scars? Time heals our wounds. It presses yesterday further away and brings us one step closer to tomorrow. It gives us hope to dream again, to believe again."

Kent thought about her words for a moment before responding. "Mom, sometimes I think you missed your calling."

Her eyes narrowed in confusion. "What do you mean?"

"I mean," he looked at her with as serious a face as he could manage, "that you should have been the preacher, not me."

She chuckled then responded with a hint of laughter in her voice. "Are you kidding me? I can't imagine handling a job like that. No, thank you!" Her expression suddenly grew quite serious. "But I know that you can because you were called to this. God called you to lead this particular flock, and you answered the call. I'm so proud of you, and so blessed and honored that you love the Lord and serve Him with your whole heart."

Kent shook his head in disbelief. "The whole thing just boggles my mind, especially when I think of where I've come from."

"It shouldn't." She took him by the hand. "Look to the Bible as your example. God took ordinary men—men who had made mistakes, no less—and used them. That's how He works. If we waited for Him to use perfect people, we'd be waiting a mighty long time."

"You're right. He's a God of second chances." *Thank You, Lord. Thank You for not giving up on me during the teen years. Thank You for not giving up on Josh Ebert. Thank You for not letting me give up on Charity during the terrible twos. Thank You for giving a second chance at love. Thank You for bringing Shauna into my life and for giving me the courage to dream again, to hope again. You are an awesome God!*

His mother looked him in the eye. "And He'll give you even more chances when you make mistakes in the future. His grace is sufficient, even for that."

Kent nodded in understanding. "That's what gets me through. That, and the love of the people in this church." His heart swelled as he thought about the people in his congregation. Young and old, they had embraced him with their love, their understanding, and their enthusiasm.

"They love you," she said. "I hear their comments. They're amazed at all you've accomplished in such a short time. And they adore Shauna. She'll make a perfect pastor's wife."

"I agree." *How could anyone not love her? She's unbelievable.*

"Her love for children is evident. You should see how many toddlers you've got in attendance today."

Kent chuckled. "Should make things exciting."

"No doubt. But speaking of children, did Shauna say how she felt about your suggestion to start a Mothers' Day Out program at the church next year?"

"She loved it." Kent couldn't help but smile as he remembered Shauna's joyful expression. "And she'll make an awesome director."

"I'm sure of it. When I see how wonderful she is with Charity, I can't help but think she'll make an awesome mother, as well."

"She will." He smiled. "But even if she struggles a little with that, it won't make any difference. She loves Charity, and that's what matters."

"Speaking of Charity," his mother interjected, "did you remember to pack her bag?"

"Yes. And I can't thank you and Andrew enough for keeping her while we're on our honeymoon."

"It's not Charity I'm worried about." His mother groaned. "It's that new puppy of hers."

Kent grinned. "He'll grow on you. I'm sure of it."

"That may take some doing, but if you say so. . ."

The door swung open and five anxious groomsmen entered the room, faces blazing with excitement. Kent couldn't help but wonder what they had been up to. His mother said her good-byes and turned to walk out of the door.

Kent's heart beat with excitement as he faced his friends. They spent a few moments together in prayer with his friend and mentor Pastor Meeks leading the way. As they walked together toward the sanctuary, Kent brushed tears from his eyes. How could he contain such joy?

&.

Shauna fumbled at the iridescent pearl buttons on the back of her white lace wedding dress. The organist began the familiar music.

"Are you ready?" Her father beamed with pride as he reached to take her by the arm.

Shauna nodded with a full heart. She had always dreamed of a June wedding. And a big church wedding, no less! "Thank you, Jesus!" she whispered.

As the doors to the sanctuary opened, the somewhat-nervous bride let her gaze focus on Kent. Her heart skipped a beat, anticipating the moment when they would be husband and wife. God had given her the desires of her heart—a husband and a precious daughter.

Kent had already taken his place at the front. He looked more handsome than she could have imagined. His eyes widened as Shauna made her way down the aisle in the white Victorian lace dress.

"New beginnings. . ." the Holy Spirit whispered to her heart.

Shauna marched slowly, methodically, eyes twinkling beneath the lace veil. Kent's mother and father sat in the front pew, holding little Charity.

"Mama!" the youngster shouted loudly as Shauna passed by.

Several members of the congregation let out a chuckle. A few even laughed out loud.

"*Shh!*" Laura Dougherty warned, putting her finger over Charity's lips.

Shauna winked at the precious little girl who was soon to become her own daughter. "I love you," she whispered.

Charity giggled and hid her face behind her hands. "Wub you!"

Shauna fought to stay focused, though the giggles of her many students kept a smile on her face. *Who cares if they're a little disruptive?* She loved them all and wouldn't have let this day go by without even one.

Pastor Meeks took his place front and center as Shauna's father placed her hand in Kent Chapman's. "The scriptures tell us 'Two are better than one, because they have a good return for their work,'" the elderly pastor reminded the congregation. "And that's why we're here today. These two are about to become one in the eyes of the Lord."

For the next few minutes, Shauna lost all track of time. She also lost track of those around her. Her gaze met Kent's in a magical connection. His eyes seemed to dance with joy.

She and Kent shared handwritten vows publicly, each pouring out their heart to the other. The carefully crafted vows brought tears to the eyes of many in attendance, but Shauna and Kent shared something far more intimate between the two of them. They shared a private communication that superseded anything yet spoken.

"I'm really no good at putting words on paper." She could practically hear Kent speaking the now-familiar phrase.

Oh, yes you are. She sent the message through her smile. *I can read your heart right now, and I love what I'm reading.*

"You may kiss the bride." The pastor spoke the anticipated

words, but it was too late. Kent had already taken her in his arms, their hearts and souls linked. They shared the joy of the moment as the pastor continued on, "I would like to introduce Mr. and Mrs. Kent Chapman."

The congregation began to celebrate aloud. The couple faced the crowd, and Shauna's heart soared. From the front row, her beautiful daughter let out a squeal and sprang from the pew to join them at the front of the church. Kent attempted to scold the youngster but seemed unable to calm her down. He looked at Shauna with an apologetic shrug.

Shauna took advantage of the opportunity to reach down and scoop up Charity, her *sweet* Charity. With her daughter's arms encircling her neck and her husband's hand firmly clasped in her own, they made their way down the aisle—stepping out of the past and into the future.

A Letter To Our Readers

Dear Reader:

In order that we might better contribute to your reading enjoyment, we would appreciate your taking a few minutes to respond to the following questions. We welcome your comments and read each form and letter we receive. When completed, please return to the following:

Fiction Editor
Heartsong Presents
PO Box 719
Uhrichsville, Ohio 44683

1. Did you enjoy reading *Sweet Charity* by Janice Thompson?
   ❏ Very much! I would like to see more books by this author!
   ❏ Moderately. I would have enjoyed it more if

   _____

   _____

   _____

2. Are you a member of **Heartsong Presents**?   ❏ Yes   ❏ No
   If no, where did you purchase this book? _____

   _____

3. How would you rate, on a scale from 1 (poor) to 5 (superior), the cover design? _____

4. On a scale from 1 (poor) to 10 (superior), please rate the following elements.

   ____ Heroine   ____ Plot
   ____ Hero   ____ Inspirational theme
   ____ Setting   ____ Secondary characters

5. These characters were special because? _____

_____

_____

6. How has this book inspired your life? _____

_____

_____

7. What settings would you like to see covered in future
   Heartsong Presents books? _____

_____

_____

8. What are some inspirational themes you would like to see
   treated in future books? _____

_____

_____

9. Would you be interested in reading other **Heartsong
   Presents** titles? ❏ Yes ❏ No

10. Please check your age range:

    ❏ Under 18   ❏ 18-24
    ❏ 25-34   ❏ 35-45
    ❏ 46-55   ❏ Over 55

Name _____

Occupation _____

Address _____

City, State, Zip _____